PECULIAR CHICKENS

A Wee Yarn for the Grands

D Malone McMillan

ISBN:
ISBN 978-1-7320062-3-2 (Paperback)
ISBN 978-1-7320062-4-9 (Ebook)

To my greatest accomplishments, Keara, Boo Bear, DJ, Gabe, ADW, Addy Malone, Davis, Emma G and Player(s) to be named later. I love you all more than words can possibly convey. A special thanks to ADW for suggesting I write a book he could read before he could vote.

CHAPTER ONE

A bicycle to a ten-year-old boy is so much more than the sum of its parts: white-walled rubber tires, shiny chrome wheels, gnarly cherry-red frame and vinyl banana seat. A bike, well ... it's freedom. Maybe this was true more back in the late Sixties, before "helicopter parents" wandered the planet in electric-powered cars, when the only rules were don't take candy from strangers and be home by supper time. Almost all our rules seemed to center around the do's and don'ts of food consumption.

A bike expanded our world from just a couple of blocks to several miles. We could reach the dark forests of Fulwood Park. The park was a dozen acres covered with tall pines that shaded the hot summer sun. It was crisscrossed with azalea-lined lovers' lanes and deep, open stormwater ditches, and aptly punctuated with wooden picnic tables, semi-functional playground gadgets and stone monuments. The park was the perfect place to play out our politically incorrect good-guy, bad-guy games. We reenacted adventures from the town's only movie theater or the Sunday afternoon matinée on television.

Things were different in your Papi's day. Not better, not worse, just different. The internet was not even a dream, and we ate apples instead of planting our adorable faces in their screens for hours on end. Cable TV was around, but just for the rich folks that could afford to pay an extra six dollars a month to receive another five grainy channels or so. Our phones had wires anchoring them to the hallway, where there was a special cove in the wall just for the purpose of stowing the luxurious high-tech device. Phones came in any color you fancied so long as that was black. We shared the phone line with five other families on the block. Wild, right? It was called a party line but there wasn't much fun to it. Any one of the other families could listen in on your conversation without your knowledge, and you couldn't make a phone call if they were using it.

Georgia lived next door. She was an eleven-year-old girl that Mom called advanced. Mom used her fingers to make air quotes around *advanced*. Not sure what that meant but Georgia made my palms leak and my brain short out. I seemed to lose my mind and say and do ridiculous stuff when she was in my immediate vicinity.

Georgia used the phone a lot. Didn't really bother me so much as my dad. He depended on customers calling him for work and him calling them to pester them for money owed. It was his unwavering opinion that children should not be allowed to use the phone "'cept in the case of emergency." And like cable TV and private phone lines, air conditioning was for the rich folks that lived in the giant brick homes north of the hospital above 20th Street.

Perspective. It's a mighty big word. Simply put, it means you look at things differently based on your experiences and your current position. We were poor. That was our experience and position. We always had been poor, so we really did not realize it. From where we sat we were just normal, run-of-the-mill folk. It's like being born blind. Can you miss sight if you never knew it? Both sets of my grandparents were sharecroppers. Sharecroppers are dirt-poor row farmers who work someone else's land for a meager share of the crops they produce. Nothing screams freedom like a twenty-hour work day in the hot Georgia sun for the outside chance of not starving in the winter.

My dad, your great-grandfather, was a housepainter. He was a hard man, fast with the belt and slow with a kind word, but he worked hard and provided for us. We never went hungry or without medical care. Mom worked as the lunch lady when I was in elementary school. I thought it was cool when I was in the first and second grade. "Look, guys. That lady in the hairnet serving us lukewarm applesauce is my mom!" You can see how perspective might change that opinion as I grew older. Later she worked as a grocery store cashier.

Your great-grandmother was a saint. She was slow with the belt and quick with the kind word. Grands, be like your great-grandmother. She ran interference with my dad for my sister and me. She worked eight-hour days, then came home to cook and clean for the family. Neither Mom or Dad finished high school. But don't for a minute think either of them to be dumb or ignorant or whatever word is acceptable to your parental units these days that means the same thing. Like I said, it was different times.

In spite of Dad's ease to anger, I had a great early childhood. Two of my cousins, Kenny and Steve, lived nearby. They were just a little older and now, with the bike, both were within comfortable range. A kid named Brian lived right behind me. He was a bit of a jerk. A know-it-all with a big mouth. But we liked him anyway or at least tried to. In fact, almost every house within a couple miles had kids close to my age. We could field two baseball teams or a platoon of good and bad guys almost any day after school, weekends or in the summer.

We didn't miss the internet or tablets or even air conditioning because we had never known those frills. That whole perspective thing. Try to always keep that in mind when your judge the past or other people. Don't judge history with a modern viewpoint lest you be judged as well. I know. That makes no sense to you right now. Maybe you will read this again when you are fifty and your kids' and grandkids' generations are judging your past harshly.

We also did not miss church. You probably know by now Papi is not a regular churchgoing man. As a kid, though, you can bet my scrawny behind was on those straight-back pine pews whenever the church doors creaked open. Church was my dad's jam. The Bible was Gospel. The pews were hard and the sermons unbearably long. There was no kids' church then. We sat with the adults and suffered through the same H-E-double-hockey-sticks fire-and-brimstone rants as the adults. Seemed God was not so loving and more a vengeful dude.

Good news is, Georgia sat in the row in front of me. She flipped her hair and smiled a lot. Well ... not so much at me, but in my general direction. She had big brown eyes the size of saucepans, and something else.

I was not quite sure what it was, but it caught my eye. Maybe it was the slightly dissimilar geometry. I was on the cusp, the edge of disliking all things girls and something mysterious I could not get my arms around. Figured it out later in life. You will too. Perspective. It is a big word and I can't spell it either. And the whole God thing, kids—your Papi believes in God ... just maybe not the vengeful one your great-granddad and Preacher introduced him too. Listen to your parents on this one for now. You can figure your version of God out later on your own.

Along with Fulwood Park our bikes brought Tyson Park within comfortable range. Tyson was a small baseball field, ill-suited for its purpose, but conveniently located as it was centered and a relaxed ride for us all. Baseball was king when I grew up. It was the game we all played and loved.

Along the third-base line ran a deep ditch with steep red clay banks. The banks were as slippery as a wet bar of soap when it rained. It rained a lot. The ditch was filled with water moccasins and crawfish and, when it flooded, human-waste floaters and a raging current that could easily wash a kid away into the storm pipes never to be seen again. Any ball hit foul down the left field line was subject to its mercy and prone to a foul watery grave.

The outfield was guarded by a low-hung chain-link fence in ill repair. Just beyond the fence was a thick row of azaleas that was home to a pride of aggressive lions masquerading as raccoons, along with an armada of hissing water moccasins. The fence was a bit too close for us. Balls were expensive and consequently a precious commodity. Once we knocked the cover off a ball, we wound it in duct tape, adding a few innings. A home run out of the park or a foul ball landing in water in the ditch was an automatic out. Three outs on both accounts if you were unsuccessful in recovering the ball. Like I said—balls were expensive; money and consequently balls, rare. There are always consequences to actions, and our ground rules codified those consequences.

These rules changed the strategy of the game. Most days we only had six or so a side, so there were big holes in the field. A good pitcher would entice the batter to pull the ball foul or long in key situations, securing the automatic ground rule out.

My cousin Steve was a good pitcher. It was the sixth inning. We only played six. Bases were loaded and I was up to bat. This was one of those key situations. We were down by two runs with two outs. A base hit ties the game. A home run or foul ball pulled left loses the game. We took baseball seriously. It was our life. It was our religion. Teams changed daily but for the next twenty-four hours or so, being the winner was … well, everything. There were no trophies to display on our dresser for winning, and most certainly no trophies for the losers. The very concept of receiving a trophy for just playing the game would have been laughable.

Steve is a ginger. I think redheads are born with a chip on their shoulder. He was also a year older, and no way was he going to let his baby-faced cousin Doug— that would be your Papi—win the game while he was on the mound. It wasn't so much a mound as it was flat, but it did have a pitcher's rubber. I reached inside my t-shirt and fingered my lucky shark tooth. We took the occasional day trip to Jekyll Island where I found a small tiger shark tooth in the sand near the surf. I attached the tooth to a piece of yarn from my mother's sewing kit for a makeshift necklace. It was my treasure. Rubbing the smooth black tooth was my self-soothing mechanism.

Steve wound up and threw high inside heat, brushing me off the plate. I gave him a dirty look and retrieved the ball from the chain-link backstop. Another ground rule. The batting team played catcher for the team in the field. This rule worked with varying degrees of effectiveness based on the integrity of the man on deck—also known as the opposing team's catcher. Steve rewarded me with another pitch, brushing me farther off the plate. I threw the ball back with all my might as a statement of protest. I was not above getting in a dust-up with my cousin. He was unmoved.

The next pitch was behind my head forcing me to the ground. That was three balls, but it didn't matter. There were no walks in our game. A hit batsman was rewarded first base only if he was moved to tears, and there is no crying in baseball.

I rolled the ball back about halfway to the mound and said, "I got all day, Ginger." Steve did not like being called Ginger. "I ain't swinging at your garbage pitches." I just needed to push one to right field and two runs would score, as there was no right fielder. The first baseman played deep but if I lifted the ball over him, two, maybe three, runs would score. Steve knew I wanted a pitch outside.

Steve nodded as if confirming the pitch with his catcher and grinned an evil smile, wiping the sweat from his pale eyes. He wound up theatrically like he was going to throw pure smoke at my head. I had backed off to deep in the batter's box and was ready for him. There it was, a middle to outside pitch I could punch gently over Kenny's head at first base. I was certain it was going to be heat, but the ball seemed to never come. Despite his elaborate wind-up the ball was painfully slow, lingering in the space between the mound and the plate taunting me.

I did everything in my power to hold my hands back, but in spite of my efforts I caught the ball square and launched it long and deep over the left field fence. Steve jumped for joy. My teammates watched in dismay and frustration as the ball sailed into the azaleas far over the fence for a home run and out number three.

It was game over, but we still needed the ball. I took my wooden bat with me for protection and searched the edges of the azaleas for the lost ball. Aluminum bats, like the internet, did not exist. And, egads, Grands, we shared bats and often mitts. Only Brian wore a batting glove and he was at least three cards short of a full deck. Bases, other than home plate, were scratches in the dirt, discarded paper plates or pine cones that often led to heated arguments with Brian as to the base's exact whereabouts.

I caught a glimpse of the duct-tape-covered ball deep in the azaleas but was distracted by movement. Water moccasins frequented my nightmares but, truth be told, I should have been more scared of the rabid marauding pride of raccoons. I expect a group of raccoons is not called a pride, but bear with me—they were fierce as lions and more common to south Georgia residential areas. I paused and the movement persisted.

It was a pup. Wait. It was a litter of pups. Most scattered when they saw me, but a tiny black puppy with a white patch on his chest cowered beside the lost ball. I reached to pick him up and he growled. He was a tiny thing but with massive paws. The smallest and clearly the slowest of the litter. Or maybe, I would come to realize later, he was the bravest and the smartest. I was no expert on animals but he could not be more than two months old.

I loved dogs and wanted one badly. Dad said no. There was no reasoning with my dad. No meant no.

That was that. You questioned Dad at your own peril. Translation—your hiney was introduced to his leather work belt if you dared talk back or question his authority or opinion, no matter how utterly absurd.

I abandoned all fear of the snake and raccoon threat, reached in and lifted the pup from the azaleas. His fur was matted. A troop of fleas performed choreographed aerial circus tricks from his back. His bony ribs were his most prominent feature. He was a thing of beauty to me in spite of his filth and malnutrition. Little did I know at the time his soul was even more beautiful and he came with a special super power.

CHAPTER TWO

It was summer in south Georgia. I had on cut-off blue jean shorts. When I say cut off, I mean cut off—not hemmed store-bought denim shorts. Mom bought me Sears Roebuck store brand jeans for school. By year's end I had run through two, maybe three, iron-on patches in each of the knees, and the jeans' hem had started creeping up at the ankle. Every summer, after school ended, she took a pair of shears to my jeans, crafting my summer wardrobe. Of course, I had one pair of long dress britches for church. Some years khaki, others corduroy. I was not a slave to fashion. Some things, Grands, they never change.

Completing my wardrobe was a plain cotton t-shirt and a pair of Sears mail-order, knock-off Converse tennis shoes. I don't know why we called them tennis shoes. I had never even seen a tennis court in real life before. Scarce few in magazines or TV.

I ripped the front of my shirt and tucked it into my shorts. The puppy, waiting impatiently at my feet, raised his hind leg and peed on my fake Converse shoes. "Thanks, little dude."

At least I knew now he was a he. That would solve a potential problem. I did not know squat about the birds and the bees, or at least I did not think I did, but for sure I knew boy dogs did not give birth. I tucked the little fellow into the front of my t-shirt. Kenny waved goodbye. He lived north. Steve and Brian were saddled up and waiting to ride with me south toward our houses.

Steve asked, "What you gonna tell your daddy?"

I had yet to figure that one out. I had an hour or so before he or Mom got home from work. My older sister, Sue, would be in her room doing whatever it is older sisters do in their rooms. Girls! She was nearly four years older and "in charge" of me. What a joke.

Brian was full of ideas, none of them the least bit helpful, and all of them a bit mean-spirited. He was that friend. The one who always seemed to need to tear down others around him to feel better about himself. Later I would gain some perspective on Brian as well. I politely asked him to stay silent if he had nothing good to say. Not really. I am just trying to be a good role model for you Grands, where your moms don't beat me when they read this story. I was a good kid, but I was a kid and Brian was a jerk. Harsh forbidden words were necessary and were spoken—loudly.

Easy there, Grands. Don't get ahead of me. Cursing, especially taking the good Lord's name in vain, was more than forbidden. Mom and Dad had an entire dictionary of other words and phrases that were off limits as well.

We minded the top few but pretty much ignored the rest of the forbidden list when adults were not within earshot. I mean, come on … you gotta say fart, right? Passing gas by all the polite names—poot, cut the cheese, lay an egg, toot, rip one, flatulence, oppsie—still smelled just as bad. Fart just gives literary flavor to the smelly act. To crudely paraphrase a great writer, you will soon grow to hate, then again later in life love, "A fart by any other name would smell as rank." I said paraphrase.

Normally, once we crossed 12th Street we pedaled fast down the hill toward our house to make it up the opposing grade with less effort. Note to Moms. I know I just gave the Grands license to say "fart," but I inserted a physics lesson shortly thereafter. An object is easier to keep in motion than to start in motion. A lesson on momentum. Moms, you are welcome.

Steve and Brian took off. My new furry friend started licking my face and peed down my shirt. I was distracted and failed to pick up the required speed. About halfway up the hill I pulled to the side of the street and started walking. Steve and Brian waved goodbye as they pulled in my driveway to cross through my back yard to their houses.

I pulled my pee-soaked t-shirt off and tied it to the seat post of the bike. "What am I gonna call you, little dude? Peabody?" The puppy frowned and whimpered.

"Not a fan? Spot, as in 'see Spot run.'" It was my first reader. Seemed predictable and not terribly poetic, though. "Rover?" I asked. The puppy yawned. Had to agree. Boring. The puppy wrapped his paw around my necklace and started licking the shark tooth.

"As my first-born, someday you will inherit my treasure as your birthright, my little prince. Prince?" I asked. The puppy shrugged. "Still not excited, eh."

Naming a dog was important. If you brought a kid home without a name, the adults started whispering about something called legitimacy, occasionally throwing out a word from the top of the forbidden list. I did not know what that meant but I knew it was not good. I needed to give him a name before we got home. There was only one prince I knew and he lived in a can. Not really—but that name was Albert.

"Albert?" I asked the puppy. He licked my face. "World," I said, lifting the puppy over my head, "meet Prince Albert."

Fortunately, like every boy that age I had stashed away several large cardboard boxes. Our house sat up about three feet off the ground. Underneath made an excellent dry hiding place and storage area for treasures to be kept hidden from parental units. Cardboard boxing high upon that list. Mom hated clutter and cardboard boxes were apparently clutter to adults. Our home was a small two-bedroom frame house with asbestos-shingle siding. Again, I said different times. Dad had closed in the porch to make a third bedroom once my sister and I got too old to share a bedroom. I wasn't sure what that meant at the time. Perspective.

The porch-turned-master-bedroom was luckily at the opposite end of the house from my room where I had constructed a cardboard fortress just underneath. I could close off the entry with another box and have a place to stash Albert. Perfect plan, I thought.

No Southern home would be complete without a water hose attached to an outside spigot. Albert stank to high heaven. I was bit confused regarding this metaphor but heard Mom use it a lot to encourage me to bathe. Was Mom suggesting there were varying levels of heaven one's stink could rise to?

Albert's fur was tangled and matted. I secreted the Joy dishwashing soap from the sink and gave him a thorough bath near the back steps. He thirstily lapped up the water off the ground. I wasn't very good at this puppy parenting stuff and had not even thought he might be hungry and thirsty. I left him unattended and went in search of food.

Mom made a full breakfast every morning for us: eggs, bacon, grits with butter and homemade buttermilk biscuits, or toast when she was in a rush. The leftovers got stored in the fridge that Dad had painted dark forest green. It wasn't a style statement. He had some dark green Rust-Oleum left over from another job. The fridge was rusting. Problem, meet solution.

I snagged a biscuit and some eggs from the fridge. I added grape jelly and a pat of butter before cutting the biscuit up in small pieces. It looked tasty so I took a bite … then another, before bringing it outside on one of Mom's ceramic plates. I poured some milk over it. The milk pooled around the edges.

The Prince attacked the plate, and before I could sit, the meal was devoured, the plate licked clean. He sat in front of me and started barking. I had not thought about the barking. I returned for another biscuit and a cereal bowl of milk. He devoured those as well.

Dad would be home any minute. I could explain the missing food but not the milk. I hated milk. More than hate. Dad had tried to make me drink it, but hard as I tried I would throw up every time even with the looming threat of a spanking. And he would notice the missing food. Dad inventoried food as if it was gold. But, come to think of it, food was more valuable than gold. I staged an accidental milk spill to cover the missing milk, being careful to leave visible evidence. I would have to go without dinner and likely take a licking, but that was a daily thing anyhow. If not for this, there would have been something else I did wrong. At least I felt this cause worthy.

Fortunately, puppies like to sleep. Albert fell fast asleep in my lap. I stashed him in my under-the-house secret fort, blocking the opening with a dirt-filled cardboard box. I kissed him on his adorable head and promised I would check on him after my parents turned in for the night.

Dad, as expected, missed the food and milk but I avoided the spanking. He must have had a good day at work. I did forfeit dinner, but Mom snuck me a baloney and cheese sandwich in my room and a glass of sweet iced tea. I saved half of the sandwich for Albert. I drank the tea. She did ask about the missing bowl. I shrugged. This was going to be harder than I thought. One lie kept leading to another lie. Lying was not in my nature and as such was pretty difficult. I wondered just how anyone could remember all their lies and not cross them up. Liars needed a good memory and that was not a strong suit for me. Seemed like telling the truth was easier, but if I told the truth I would lose Albert, and in spite of our short time together I was pretty fond of the little fellow.

Summer in south Georgia is brutally hot. We slept with our windows open and on top of the white cotton sheets. When there was a breeze it was manageable. All the neighbors had their windows open. Late at night when it got quiet you could catch scraps of conversations from other houses drifting on the warm breeze. There weren't many secrets in our neighborhood, at least in the summer. Tonight, you could also hear the unmistakable sound of a puppy whimpering.

Darn, I thought. I grabbed my penlight from the dresser drawer, unfastened the screen and slithered out my bedroom window. The half-eaten baloney sandwich was still wrapped in wax paper and was tucked in a pocket in my shorty PJ bottoms. I did not wear a shirt to bed. I peeked under the house, expecting darkness, but there was light.

"What the heck?" I mumbled. Technically, heck was on the list of forbidden words, but like a tree falling in the forest, if no one heard it, did it really make a sound? I duck-walked back to the light, wishing I had remembered my pocketknife. Yes, these were different times, Grands. I had a hand-me-down pocketknife, a hatchet and a Bowie knife. And, no, your moms will not let you have one.

Albert was squeaking and jumping around. Someone I could not make out was with him. It was a girl and she was shushing him and had yet to notice me. I paused, gathering my thoughts and formulating an appropriate strategy to address the clear and present danger. There was a girl of unknown origins in my secret fort. Unacceptable! This was anarchy. Before I could formulate the appropriate response, Albert broke loose and charged me, digging in my PJ pockets for the baloney sandwich.

"Doug. What on earth are you doing here at this time of night?" She went straight to the offensive.

Her strategy worked. I was confused and threw out a convenient lie. "I heard a noise." Wait a minute, I thought. This is my house and my dog. Who and why is this creature under my house playing with my puppy and why am I explaining myself to this intruder of my secret fort? Is there not anything sacred? I shined my flashlight into her face. She covered her face with her arm, but I recognized her.

"Georgia?" My newfound bravery turned to something else. I wasn't scared of her, but she sure scared me.

"Yes, Doug."

Wait—what? She knew my name. She was an older girl and one of the few from our neighborhood on the "A" list. Cheerleader, student council, cool kids lunch table. What new mysterious world had I just entered in the dark space underneath my bedroom?

CHAPTER THREE

Even in the summer, morning came early in our house. The smell of breakfast usually caught my attention well before the sun made its grand entrance. Mom kissed my forehead about ten minutes before I had to get up. I took those kisses for granted. You know, Grands ... I would give just about anything in the world for one of those kisses about now. Cherish your moms while you can. Okay, Moms ... am I out of your doghouse for issuing the fart license now?

Mom would yell down the hall as she was setting the table, giving us final notice to crawl out of bed and join Dad for breakfast.

Dad shoveled a forkful of fried egg into his mouth with as much grace as a one-legged man playing hopscotch in mismatched high-heeled shoes. Picture the problems with that metaphor. He held his one good eye suspiciously on me. I was feeling guilty and worried Albert might start barking once he smelled the food and heard the commotion. I had crawled back into my bed a little after midnight, leaving Albert sleeping in Georgia's lap. I was more than a little jealous, yet fell fast asleep dreaming of puppies frolicking in the sand and did not hear a peep out of either of them.

Dad was Scottish and had one remarkable green eye and one dull blind one. His eyes were heavily guarded with a single bushy eyebrow prematurely graying. He had this disturbing habit of twisting a spidery eyebrow hair between his forefinger and thumb when he was in deep thought. On occasion, he forcefully plucked one out and examined the hair in the light as if it held some singular mystic knowledge. He was twisting his eyebrow hairs.

"Son, you up to no good." It was not a question.

"No, sir." I looked down at my plate. I had sectioned off half my plate to save for Albert. It was not a lie. Taking care of an abandoned puppy was surely good. Dad plucked a hair from his brow and held it up squinting into the light.

"Hazy, try again," I mumbled.

"What?" Dad furrowed his brow.

You need to borrow my magic 8-ball? I thought the words but wisely kept the wisecrack to myself as I did not have an 8-ball anyway. Instead, I replied, "Is it going to be hazy today?" Dad grunted, discarding the mystical hair on the floor.

Mom only sat at the table for a moment before continuing her chores. She always laid out my clothes for the day, even in summer when it was pretty much cut-off blue jeans and a plain cotton t-shirt every day. I was her baby, with no prospect of a future child. Looking back, I think she was holding on tightly. She came back into the dining room and paused to give me a knowing look before moving to the sink to begin cleaning the kitchen.

She eyed my half-eaten plate. "Not hungry this morning, son?" I was always hungry. This was universal knowledge. It was like there was a monster in my belly that devoured everything I sent his way, pooped, and then immediately began demanding resupply. She took my plate and covered it in Saran wrap, not bothering to place it in the fridge with the remaining leftovers. Grands, moms are a darn sight brighter than they let on.

I scurried to my room to make my bed and change clothes. In the dim lamp light, I noticed my sheets were smudged with red clay stains. I looked at my feet and knees to see the unmistakable telltale signs of Georgia red clay as well. I was digging myself a deeper hole.

Quick as I made the bed I jumped into my clothes and tossed my PJ s in the hamper. There were revealing smudges of clay all over them, along with grains of sand in the pockets and short black hairs shed from Albert. Deeper still I dug.

Mom and Dad left shortly, with Mom admonishing me to get my chores done "'fore I went off to play." I nodded. She kissed my forehead.

Sue disappeared into her room, but I was gonna need her help as I needed to wash my bedsheets and my PJs to destroy the evidence of my late-night excursion. Sue was charged with the inside chores; me, the outside. It was the standard division of labor in the Sixties. For sure, us boys got the better end of that deal.

First things first—I needed to check on Albert. The sun was yet to rise but it was fairly light out. I took the penlight anyway as I was not a fan of the dark. I was expected to get dirty in the daytime so I need not be careful. I hastily made my way under the house to my fort. Shining the light in front of me, I noticed the makeshift gate to the fort was not in place. I scurried the few remaining feet, panicked to find Albert had escaped. I noticed a note taped to fort's wall, scrawled in perfect penmanship: "Albert is with me." She had drawn a heart and signed it "your new friend, Georgia." She dotted the "i" in her name with a heart.

Based on conversation the night before, I had found out Georgia's dad was the night security guard for a local cold storage plant on the edge of town. It was a giant sprawling refrigerated warehouse. Companies rented out space in the warehouse to keep products there that needed to stay cold. He worked most nights patrolling the complex, getting home a little after eight a.m.

Her mom stayed in her room drinking boxed wine that she called "mommy juice" and watching TV. She slept with the random sound and light from the static of the TV after the local station signed off for the night. I was no expert on wine. The only wine I had had was at communion and it came from a Welch's grape juice bottle. We were good Southern Baptists. Jesus, he turned the water into grape juice. I could only speculate Georgia was a Methodist. Dad made a joke about the only difference between Methodists and Baptists was that Methodists said hello to each other in the liquor store.

Georgia's front door was open. I tapped lightly on the screen door so as not to wake anyone. The screen fell open as I cupped my hands against it to peer inside. Most people slept with the door open but did latch the screen for at least the appearance of security. Georgia was curled up on the wooden floor sleeping on a pallet with Albert on her belly. I shook her shoulder gently but she did not wake. I heard movement from the back.

Her mother called out, "Georgia, is that you stirring? Be a darling and bring your mama a cup of coffee." Her mom had that unmistakable gravelly voice of a lifelong smoker. I swiftly gathered up Albert and made my way outside before I was discovered and dug a new hole adjacent to the rather deep one I already had going.

It took a village to raise a dog. Dogs had free rein. I don't think I even knew what a dog leash was. A few homes were fenced, but even those often kept the gates open. Wasn't much traffic on our road, but on the sad occasion a dog got run over, we gave it a good Christian burial in the empty lot across the street. Preacher said dogs did not go to heaven, but I knew that was a lie. People often left water and food on their porch for the dogs, cats both feral and domesticated, and unfortunately the pride of rabid marauding raccoons.

I wasn't the least bit worried about Albert in the daytime. The neighbors all looked after the kids and the animals. It was just at night I was concerned. He was too little to be left alone and, like me, probably scared of the dark—not to mention the roaming pride of raccoons. That was a thing.

I scraped the remainder of breakfast off the plate onto the porch steps and filled the cereal bowl with water from the hose. Albert devoured the other half of my breakfast and licked my hand wanting more.

"Dude. You had as much breakfast as me, boy." Guess he had a ravenous monster in his belly as well.

"Quit your belly-aching. I'll share with him," Georgia said as she walked around the corner. She was barefoot and had her dark hair tied neatly in a ponytail. She had a bowl of Cheerios in one hand, a bottle of milk in the other.

Some folks still got their milk delivered to them each morning on the front porch in glass bottles with little paper tabs covering the opening. You could buy paper-carton milk from the store, but Mom brought home milk from school. She did not steal it. Nothing like that. Some of the kids, like me, returned unopened milk cartons on their trays. It was supposed to go in the garbage, but the cafeteria ladies would have none of that waste. They shared the returned milk among themselves.

Georgia tossed out the water and poured half her milk bottle into the bowl. She ate a couple of bites of cereal and placed the remainder of her cereal on the wooden steps. Albert made quick work of both.

"Who names their kid Georgia?" I asked. It was an unusual name, but more importantly I was trying to regain the leverage I had never possessed with this creature.

Georgia scoffed. "Clearly my parents."

"Well, what kind of name is that?"

She flushed a bit, but said, "I was born in Savannah."

"Okay. I was born in Tifton and my name ain't Georgia. What's your point?"

"My mom filled out the birth certificate one line off."

I looked at her, confused.

"Are you a bit touched?" Georgia asked me.

I shrugged. She continued, "Mom wrote in the city and state I was born in where she was supposed to write first and middle name."

I laughed. I made the same mistake all the time with forms at school. "So, Georgia is your middle name."

She smiled and nodded. "Maybe you are only a little touched. And Savannah is my first name." She looked at me, daring me to laugh.

"Savannah, Georgia. I kinda like it." And I did. More importantly, I saw no benefit in picking around her sore spot. I did secretly wonder if her official place of birth was Mary Ann or Betty Lou.

"He needs a flea collar," Georgia said, changing the subject while scratching Albert behind his ears. They were exceptionally soft, Albert's ears. She was correct. In spite of the bath, fleas were still doing circus tricks from the fur on his back.

"Where do I get one of them?"

"Dalton's," she responded.

Dalton's was a neighborhood store about two miles from our house. It was somewhere between what you might call a grocery store and a department store, but all on a small scale. Later Dalton added self-serve gas pumps when they became the rage. Big-box retail stores eventually ran him out of business, much like Amazon will run the big-box retail stores out of business soon enough. In the back of the store was the butcher shop, where the store's namesake, Dalton, sliced meat and held court. In the front, Shirley, his wife, was on the cash register. Their son, about my sister's age, worked whenever school was out, stocking the shelves and sweeping the aisles. Almost all kids got an after-school and summer job once they turned twelve.

"How much you reckon a flea collar costs?" I asked Georgia.

She shrugged. "Dunno. I have a little money saved up. I can help."

"Okay. Wanna ride over after chores?" I asked. I was relieved she offered. I had nearly two dollars saved up, but I needed to buy a new baseball. We were down to two balls—both on their last legs wrapped in duct tape. One was seriously waterlogged as well from a long trip down the foul ditch.

Kenny darn near drowned trying to retrieve that ball. It had rained a lot and the water was raging in the ditch with the floaters sailing along at breakneck speeds. It was late in the game, there were no outs and Kenny's team was losing when he yanked the ball foul into the ditch. Of course, he jumped into the rushing waters to retrieve the ball with no thought for his own safety. The current pushed him under the road into the pitch-black darkness of the culvert. He got hung up on some debris and we weren't sure he was ever gonna come out the other side.

We were about to call it a day and go home when he popped out the far side but lost control of the ball. I jumped in to save the ball. Like I said, balls were rare. They still lost the game, but through no fault of Kenny's.

It was a wonder we had not all died from staph infections, water-hose poisonings, sugar overdoses, or secondhand cigarette smoke as a kid. I think maybe kids are a bit more rugged than currently given credit.

Georgia nodded yes, she would ride with me to Dalton's. I was going on my first date and did not even know it.

CHAPTER FOUR

Our system of shared puppy parenthood worked out well for the remainder of the summer. Georgia kept Albert every night with her, and the entire community minded to Albert during the day. He was the neighborhood favorite, full of life, friendly and always up for a game of fetch, a wrestling match, a meal or bowl of milk. He was getting pretty fluffy. I wondered if he was aware of those starving children in China. We had no way of knowing for certain, but we thought he might be a cross between a black lab and a Rottweiler. As he got bigger he started running with a curious tilt as if his frame was off kilter. Albert liked to wrestle, and his signature move was to stand on his back legs, place his paws on your shoulders and twist you to the ground. We decided there was some black bear mixed into his ancestry. Confused on bear species we named his signature wrestling move the Grizzly.

Each morning Georgia brought Albert by before her dad got home, and we shared our breakfast with him. It was my favorite part of the day. School was starting soon and I was curious if Georgia would "know" me at school. Everybody liked me but I wasn't a cool kid like Georgia.

It may have been the best summer of my youth except for the dreams. I dreamed of puppies every night. At first, they were all good dreams; then they turned a little dark. I know it's crazy, but Albert seemed to narrate my dreams … not in words, but with a series of pictures, like a slideshow telling a story.

It was a Saturday night, late, when I woke up with a start from one of those dreams. The sheet was soaked from my sweat. I gasped for breath and reached for my pocketknife. Someone was at my window. I peeked outside to see Georgia standing in the light of the full moon on tiptoes at my window with Albert at her bare feet. I can't think of a more beautiful sight that I had ever seen. Wait—what? I did not like girls. They had cooties. Even Georgia with her cute freckles, crooked smile and massive brown eyes. Oh, no, I thought.

"Doug," she urged. "Wake up. We have an emergency." Albert whined, gave a low growl and stood on his back legs like a circus bear.

I nodded, wiped the sleep from my eyes and pulled on a t-shirt. "Right there." I needed to pee and more importantly fart. Mom explained I should never "pass gas in mixed company." She did not explain as to why. I thought maybe farts were the equivalent of kryptonite to girls. Boy, did your Grinnie ever prove me wrong.

I already knew what this was about. One of Albert's siblings was in trouble. The Malvados lived two doors down from Georgia, right next to the big ditch that ran perpendicular to our street. They were trouble. Their yard was a field of weeds interrupted by the rare blade of brave overgrown grass. Two broken-down vehicles, set up on concrete blocks, framed their drive. A rusted-out engine block always hung from a giant live oak, waiting for repairs that would never come.

There were at least six Malvado kids, all boys. I say at least because they were elusive rascals and hard to count. Three of them, of varying ages, were in the same grade with me when they chose to show up for school. Three were in high school but had dropped out. An uncle lived with them, who had just got out of jail for what Mom said was drunken and disorderly conduct. Not sure what that meant. Pretty sure Georgia's mom got drunk every night, but her conduct was to pass out in front of the TV. Not too much disorder in a good nap. She never hurt anyone except by what Preacher called the sin of omission. That means not doing something you were supposed to.

All the lights were blazing, and hillbilly music was blaring from the radio at a level that far exceeded the design parameters of the device. It was the middle of summer but they had a huge bonfire in the back yard. There must have been a couple of dozen of them sitting around the fire, passing a bottle between them and spitting in the fire.

Georgia pointed to the edge of the fire. There he was. A skinny, matted, black lab mix much like Albert, chained to the oak tree with the rusted engine block. I could not hear him for the distorted music blaring from the radio, but I could tell he was whimpering. Albert growled.

Georgia rolled up her sleeves and spat in both hands. Darn, I thought. Did I have a crush on this girl? I wiped my face and mumbled to myself, "Get a grip, Doug. Work needs doing."

Georgia looked at me and shrugged. "What?"

She took off to run into the fray. I grabbed her arm and pulled her down beside me a little harder than I intended. No one had seen us yet. I wanted to keep it that way. "What's your plan?" I asked.

She shrugged. "I dunno. Go rescue the dog. Duh."

The "duh" was a little hurtful. "There is a thin line between bravery and stupidity," I explained. I don't remember which war movie I stole the line from, but I continued showing off my extensive knowledge of Hollywood battle tactics. "But attacking a fortified position without superior numbers and without a plan is suicide."

Albert barked but there was no danger the Malvados heard him.

It was an early lesson for me. Girls, especially the cute ones, could get a boy in a whole mess of trouble. I expect I just lost some Mom points here, but I am truth-telling. Grandsons, be careful. I'll leave it at that for now. Come see me without your moms when you turn fifteen and we can be more direct.

I turned to Georgia, still eager to implement a full-frontal assault despite being outnumbered and outgunned. Maybe I had watched a World War II movie or two too many. Several nights over the summer I had snuck out and spent the evening with Georgia playing with Albert on her living room floor. Her mom was oblivious by ten p.m. or so from her mommy juice. I figured the bottle the Malvados were passing would have a similar effect. I suggested, "Strategic patience."

"What on earth are you talking about?" Georgia asked.

"We do nothing and wait for them to go to sleep."

"Nothing. That is your grand plan? Boys!" she mumbled under her breath.

I miscalculated. Georgia shook me awake. I am not sure how long I slept, but the moon had moved a long distance in the sky. Half the Malvados were still around the fire and the music was still blaring some tune about drinking, cheating, grandma, dogs, reindeers, trains, honky-tonks, dirt roads, barns and pickup trucks.

"What is your grand plan now, genius?"

"Ouch!" I recognized the stinging sarcasm. Albert licked my face and growled. "Whose side are you on, you furry Benedict Arnold?" See, Moms, how I worked a history lesson into the story as well? Further out of the Mom hole I climb.

Albert, impatient, took the initiative and ran straight into the middle of the Malvados. Catching them off guard, he attacked the largest Malvado of those still awake, grabbing his pants legs and aggressively dragging him toward the fire. Albert was only thirty or forty pounds by now and still a puppy, but with surprise and naked aggression he had created a diversion for us.

We scampered to our feet and ran for the chained puppy. Georgia broke left. I took the right flank. Georgia executed a perfect baseball slide in to the puppy and began to remove the chain. One of the older Malvados grabbed a burning log off the fire and took a wild swing at Albert but missed and caught another Malvado square in the no-nos. Words I cannot repeat were spoken.

Fortunately, in the confusion, most of the Malvados had taken to fighting each other but the wily old uncle spotted me out of the side of his eye. He had not shaved or bathed in what I expect had been weeks. I could smell and feel his sour breath. I smiled and waved as if I was not in possession of the entirety of my faculties.

It was my go-to move, one Mom and my elementary school principal strongly disapproved.

"You little brat," he roared. It was nothing like that really. He said words that literally burned my earholes. I have ear scars to this day. Ask your Papi to see them. I thought if Jesus were listening, he might at that very moment strike that vile man dead. He did not.

Georgia yelled, "Duck," as she tossed a monkey wrench at the uncle. Her aim was true and the wrench found its intended mark, square on his unshaven face with the unmistakable sound of teeth breaking. He smiled, blood trickling from his mouth. Not the expected response.

Georgia yelled, "Run." I thoughtfully obliged. Fortunately, the uncle did not give enthusiastic chase.

We ran up the street away from our house and cut across PK's yard in order to double back through Brian's. Albert led the way with the new puppy on his tail. Georgia went inside to get some food. We were quick learners after all. I found some dish soap and a hose. The little fellow smelled. Shortly Georgia joined me with the food.

Brian made his way over virtually on our heels. "What the Sam Hill are you guys doing?"

"Does anybody sleep in this neighborhood?" I asked.

Brian stuttered, "You guys woke me stumbling though my yard ... like a pride of marauding rabid raccoons." I told you that was a thing.

I eyed Brian suspiciously. He was fully dressed, including socks and shiny new metal baseball cleats, and was not more than a minute behind us. Not many of us had cleats. The ones who did had rubber ones, likely duct-taped-together hand-me-downs from older brothers. Metal cleats were for the high school team.

Georgia had brought out a flashlight to examine the puppy and shined it briefly at Brian. His left eye was black, his lip split, and his glasses were taped together with Scotch tape.

"What is this?" I asked.

He shrugged. "I fell."

I looked at his broken glasses and pointed. "Maybe a more practical gift for falling, you think?"

The puppy crawled into Brian's lap, still soaking wet from his bath. Albert joined him, aggressively licking the new puppy. There was no doubt these two dogs were siblings. Georgia found no major wounds, just a few shallow cuts on the puppy. Brian started sobbing.

"You crying?" I asked.

Georgia elbowed me hard in the side. Girls, at least in my day, were much more sensitive than boys. Modern scholars assert this is a learned behavior. Your Papi strongly disagrees. We are wired differently to perform different tasks, and it's the very complement of those differences that has ensured the survival of our species. But that is all for another day.

"No. I'm not crying," Brian responded, tears running down his swollen face. "Can I keep him?" he asked.

Georgia said, "Only if you can keep him safe. Can you keep him safe?"

I started to voice my objections. Brian was a jerk. I did not trust him with the puppy and I sure did not trust his dad. Georgia elbowed me again hard in the side. "That one is gonna leave a mark," I said, rubbing my side.

"Quit your crying," Georgia mumbled to me. Maybe she wasn't wired that differently after all.

Brian started sobbing. I was ten. This was a lot for me. Boys just did not cry. The only time I cried was when my dad spanked me, because I knew he would stop as soon as I started bawling. I think he knew this trick, but it was the equivalent of me tapping out or calling "uncle."

Georgia held Brian in her arms while he sobbed. I was more than a little bit jealous and even more confused as to why. We were just a few feet removed from my parents' bedroom and their light suddenly switched on. I shushed them.

Brian checked his watch and reached out to show me its luminous dial. "Holy Moses. It's six a.m." We had been out all night. Brian gathered up the puppy.

Georgia hugged Brian one last time and took Albert in her arms.

"What you gonna name her?" she asked. It had become self-evident the new puppy was a she during her frequent bathroom breaks.

Brian thought for a minute, turned and smiled. "I'm gonna name her Hope. Yeah, her name is Hope."

CHAPTER FIVE

I had no more than shut my eyes before I felt the kiss on my forehead. *Double dog drat,* I thought.

Mom pulled back, and a look of concern crossed her face. She felt my forehead with the palm of her hand. It was magically calibrated to the tenths to measure fever. "You have a fever, baby." It was not a question.

"No, Mom. I feel fine. Just had a restless night." No lies there. Later I learned this was called equivocation — which, truth be told, is still more or less a lie.

Mom scurried off to get the thermometer to confirm what she was already certain of. She placed the mercury-filled glass rod carefully under my tongue while pulling the sheets up about me. After a few uncomfortable minutes, she pulled out the device and squinted into the pale light. Her entire body frowned.

"Oh, my." She patted my head. "Just stay in bed this morning, baby." She brought back a cool wash rag and placed it on my forehead. It felt delightful. She handed me two Bayer aspirin and a glass of water. Aspirin and milk of magnesia were the cure-all wonder drugs available to moms of the day. I gulped the medicine down. She turned off the lamp and eased out the door.

Exhausted from the night's adventure, I dozed off, hoping I had satisfactorily scrubbed off any evidence. I was awakened by Mom's raised voice. "Your son has a fever of 103. He doesn't need church, he needs a doctor."

"The boy is goldbricking. Wake him up. Get him dressed—he is going to church," Dad shouted.

Goldbricking. I knew the term from my steady diet of war movies. It meant faking sick to get out of one's duty. I really didn't feel that bad so I tried to get up, but there it was. An intense sharp pain in my belly. I grew wings and flew to the toilet, my feet not once touching the hardwood floor on the short journey. Mercifully, our only bathroom was unoccupied. I barely cleared the seat lid before my bowels erupted in a volcanic explosion of hot molten lava the likes of which not seen since Pompeii.

"That can't be good," I mumbled. According to Mrs. Royal's biology class, that particular exit was designed for the disposal of solid waste. The sharp pain returned, but this time I evacuated a chunky toxic brew out of my mouth. I was beginning to doubt Mrs. Royal's teacher credentials. Mercifully, my aim was solid and the chunky brew found the bathtub. I cleared up my mess and crawled back to my bed. Maybe I was sick.

I never got sick. Sue, she got sick. This was something new to me. I had never missed a day of school or, as my dad saw it, more importantly, I had never missed church, including Wednesday night prayer service and the annual revival service, two revivals during droughts of rain for the collection plate. Dad was clear that my spiritual education was the priority.

Just as I got comfortable under the sheets, my bedroom door was flung open. It was Dad. "Get dressed, boy. We got church."

I dutifully complied. There was no arguing with Dad. I could hear Mom quietly sobbing in the background. I knew what I needed to do. Mom had not laid out my Sunday clothes, but I only had one pair of dress pants and two identical white button-down dress shirts. There weren't a lot of tough decisions to be made. I smartly threw on a second pair of whitey-tightie underwear for insurance. The uncontrollable hot lava eruption had me concerned for a likely unscheduled, ill-timed, repeat performance. My stomach was not to be trusted. I grabbed the starched white shirt and clipped on the paisley tie. I could not find my dress socks so I grabbed my calf-high white ones.

I washed my face and brushed my teeth before throwing up twice again and pooping once more. This was a marathon, not a sprint. My throat felt like I was swallowing razor blades and my head pounded. I looked in the mirror. "You got this, kid." I did not.

We jumped into the family car, a white Ford Galaxy 500 with blue vinyl seats. It was Dad's pride and joy. God, country, automobile, work, family was my dad's order of priorities.

Before we even got a block from the house, I felt my stomach dangerously bubbling and the sharp pain intensifying. "Mom, I have to use the bathroom." The words came out in an unrecognizable little girl's panicked voice.

Mom turned to Dad and silently raised an eyebrow.

"He can wait till we get to church," Dad said, self-assured that if he willed it so, my bowels would comply.

My stomach lurched. "No, I can't, Dad," I protested.

"Don't back-talk me, boy," he roared.

And that was that. My bowels disobeyed Dad, and I violently pooped my pants. It was all liquid and there was no mistaking the volumes of brown smelly mess shooting through the cotton confines of my safety drawers onto Dad's prized, once pristine, blue vinyl seats. Dad looked over into the back seat in disgust and barely controlled rage. Sue understandably recoiled to the farthest corner of the seat to avoid the toxic spill and Dad's livid gaze. To this day I have never again seen her look so genuinely horrified.

Mom dangerously raised an "I told you so" eyebrow. Dad swerved hard left and executed a careless U-turn in the middle of the street, squealing tires as he reversed direction.

Dad angrily paced outside the bathroom door until I finished washing. He slid off his Sunday belt and spanked me. It was a rare Sunday-belt spanking. Normally I got the work belt. Dad followed Jesus' example on Sundays and was typically a touch more merciful, though not on this day. I did not cry. Nor did I ever cry again when he spanked me. No matter how hard or how long, I vowed, I would never give in to him again. Nothing was ever the same after that day with my dad and me. Something important, almost sacred, was forever lost.

CHAPTER SIX

My fever raged through the night and as the fever rose, Albert's voice became stronger. He introduced me to all his littermates. There were seven. Most had found good homes now except for a couple. I was ten. I knew I could not save the world. I would have to wait at least until I was fifteen in order to do that. But by the grace of the almighty God, as Preacher would say, I could save those puppies.

I felt the cool rag on my forehead and a gentle caress on my cheek before I opened my eyes. "Just give me five more minutes, Mom, and I will get up." My head was throbbing and my throat felt like I was chewing on the razor-blade-laced apples Mom always fretted about on Halloween. She really had nothing to worry about. We just ate the candy and tossed the apples at street signs.

Georgia giggled. I cracked an eye open and sat up in bed. "Georgia?"

She blushed and jumped up from the bed. "Your mom asked I keep an eye on you while she called the doctor."

That seemed highly unlikely. The phone was in the hallway just outside my door. I could hear Mom on the phone asking the neighbors to "yield the line for an emergency call." She was not dialing 911. That was not a thing then.

Mom was the master of hyperbole, which is yet another kind way of saying a lie. She was a godly woman with few faults, but she tended to exaggerate. For sure I was sick, but I don't think it rose to the emergency level. Then again, she had taken off from work and was calling the doctor.

"Am I dying?" I asked, panicking just a bit. Maybe this was the one day we were warned about when Mom was not crying wolf. Grands, you know this story, as Addy will later aptly summarize it as the "you lie, you die" fable of The Boy That Cried Wolf.

Georgia giggled. "No, but if your Mom sees all those clay stains on your sheets you might wish you were."

"Dang. I forgot—"

"Forgot to what, young man?" Mom raised a thick eyebrow. "Wash the dog hair and red clay from your bed sheets?" She stood waiting for an answer with one hand on her hip.

"Yes, ma'am." I needed to put the shovel down. The hole was sufficiently deep. Georgia started to creep out of the room.

"Don't you go anywhere, little lady." My mom did have eyes in the back of her head. It was standard issue mom gear in the Sixties. "And that mouth, young man. Where do you hear those obscene words?" I thought at church mostly. The big kids hung out in the graveyard directly behind the church after service, smoked nasty cigarettes and told stories laced with a few mild obscenities and unlikely conquests. They thought they were being cool. They weren't, but I did pick up some colorful vocabulary from them. I looked at Mom and just shrugged. I did not want to throw the big kids under the bus and suffer the likely beating at their hands for ratting them out.

"What's his name?" Mom asked Georgia.

"Whose name?" Georgia stuttered. Mom gave Georgia the Mom stink eye. "Albert. His name is Albert."

Mom smiled. "What kind of silly name is Albert? How about Rover, or Spot?"

Georgia assumed the question was rhetorical and that Mom did not expect a reply. Georgia was mistaken. After an extended awkward silence, she said, "Well ... those names were taken."

Mom broke out laughing. "I guess they are, missy." I braved a smile. "You," she pointed at me, "are still in my doghouse." She smiled at her accidental pun. "Go take a bath. The doctor will be here in an hour. Georgia, why don't you introduce me to your new friend ... Albert?"

Doctoring was a lot different when I was a kid. First off, the doctor came to you. This was referred to as a house call. More importantly, you never called the doctor unless you were real sick. They were expensive but that wasn't the real reason. My parents were brought up in the Great Depression. Their parents were kids shortly after the War of Northern Aggression that you likely know as the Civil War. Self-reliance was more than just a virtue, it was a religion. You just did not accept help from other people, as it was considered dishonorable.

This was an extreme position, as there is nothing wrong with accepting assistance when you need it. Just know and appreciate that someone had to sacrifice to offer that help. Like my mom said, "There ain't no free lunch, boy. Someone had to earn it." There is shame in taking from others against their will. Call it what you might, but it is stealing, plain and simple. Always remember, there is no nobility in taking one person's money and giving it to another. Nobility comes from self-sacrifice, not inflicting sacrifice on a third party. You want to play Robin Hood, make sure you give the shirt off your back before taking someone else's.

I heard the bath water running before my feet hit the floor. Mom had laid out a fresh towel and PJs. I was shivering from the fever, and the warm water felt good against my skin. We were taught to bathe in just a couple of inches of water. Mom said it was wasteful to use more. The real reason being she could not swim and was deathly afraid of drowning. Me ... fortunately I could swim like a fish.

To this day I don't fully understand why doctors look in your ears, listen to your chest and tap your knee no matter your ailment. Seems like ceremony. Much ado about nothing except appearances. I have come to learn in my old age there is a lot of that in the world— ceremony, that is. People doing stuff to make them feel good about themselves but having no real impact on solving the problem at hand. Grands, do stuff to make a real difference, not just to make you look as if you did or to feel some false nobility. Substance over form. Don't put looking good over being good.

Georgia giggled uncontrollably. Dr. Cohen turned and eyed her over his thick bifocal glasses. She sat quietly, fearing he might reach into his dark leather black bag of torture contraptions for her next. Doc turned to Mom. "Must of picked a bug up somewhere." Let me translate: "I have no idea what is wrong with your boy."

The doctor continued, "A dose of penicillin should knock it out of him." Translation: "I am going to give your son a shot of medicine to make you think I know what I am doing, but will likely as not do nothing to help." Penicillin was a relatively new miracle drug in the day. It was an antibiotic and as such would have no effect on any virus I had picked up.

I bravely presented my arm. Georgia was watching. I don't know why, but I felt like I needed to make sure she did not know I was about to pee my PJs in abject terror at any minute. I was not a fan of needles, and penicillin meant needles.

Dr. Cohen scoffed and smiled. "No, sir." He pulled a large metal cylinder from his bag and affixed a colossal needle on the end. It was so large the United States Postal Service had granted the needle its own ZIP code. He wiped the reusable needle off with a bit of cotton soaked in alcohol in order to kill the preponderance of germs. Squinting, he filled the needle from a glass bottle of an opaque white liquid in his bag. "This here," he raised the torture apparatus to eye level, squirting out a tiny white drop from the business end of the needle, "goes in your bare bum."

Other than taking up God's mantel and entering the ministry, there was no higher calling than becoming a doctor. The usual suspects rounded out the list of respected professions: teachers, police officers, service members, nurses, plumbers … On the flip side, lawyers stood alone at the bottom as least respected and most defiled professions, with used car salesman and politicians tied at next to the last. Grands, with time your Papi has gained some wisdom. It is the person, the individual's actions, not the profession, that should make the person respected or defiled. For sure it is a statistical fact that fifty percent of all the doctors graduated in the bottom half of their class. I am pretty sure Dr. Cohen, kind-hearted as he was, fell into the bottom half.

Georgia giggled and scurried out of the room for safety prior to being exposed to my bare bum. She returned when the deed was done and the doctor had withdrawn. "Well, at least you did not cry," Georgia said or maybe it was a question.

I didn't tell her I all but peed my pants. I yawned and a fart slipped out in mixed company. The doctor had given me some cherry-flavored medicine with codeine in it to help with my pain and manage the fever. It made me sleepy. Mom did not send for a switch for my fart transgression. I wasn't sure what to make of that. Sometime later the medical profession figured out that giving codeine, an addictive narcotic, to kids was a really bad idea. Science, it is never settled, just you wait and see.

I slept through lunch and woke up famished. I took this as a good sign. Georgia was curled up on the other twin bed in my room. I heard Mom in the kitchen.

"There you are. Hungry?" I think Mom could read my mind. And that was not good. My mind was full of thoughts my mom did not need to be privy to. She placed a bowl of hot chicken noodle soup in front of me.

"Yuck. How about a peanut butter sandwich?" I asked. Next to fried chicken and french fries, a peanut butter sandwich was my favorite meal. Some days I wanted to go find George Washington Carver and shake that gentleman's hand. Chicken noodle soup, on the other hand, did not make the list of acceptable food options.

"You will eat what you are offered. There are starving children in China." Grands, do moms still use that lame guilt tactic?

She grabbed a dish of strawberry Jell-O out of the fridge and spooned me out a heathy portion. I reached for the Jell-O. While not high on the list of favored foods, Jell-O, in spite of its equestrian origins, did make the cut.

"Uh-uh. Soup, then Jell-O," Mom said, shaking her head from side to side and pointing at each dish in the acceptable order of consumption.

"How about we pack up the soup and send it to China and I just eat the Jell-O?" And, Grands, do kids still answer with an even lamer derivative of this line?

"You want I send Georgia out to find me a switch?" Mom said. I smiled; maybe I was not dying after all.

As part of Mom's punishment ritual, she would have us go out and break a thin branch off a bush, a switch, for her to spank us with. Mom's spankings were all ritual and not much pain. Sort of like your mom's time-out in the corner, Grands.

"No, ma'am." I swallowed a spoonful of soup. Before it even hit my stomach, it came back up all over the kitchen table combined with inglorious foul chunks of a meal long since forgotten. I had not eaten since supper two days past. Just how much undigested food did a ten-year-old boy's body hold?

Mom felt my head again. "Child, you are still burning up." She frowned. I felt like I disappointed her.

"Sorry, Mom."

She rubbed my closely shorn head, smiled and said, "Don't be silly, son." I loved the way she said son.

The doctor advised Mom to give me another dose of the codeine-laced medicine. I slept till the sun woke me up the next morning. Georgia was gone and I recalled it was the first day of school and I would be late.

CHAPTER SEVEN

I missed school that day and again the next. Georgia brought me my assignments and helped me with my multiplication tables. I was a smart kid but a bit of a lazy one. Okay, more than a bit, when it came to book learning. I struggled with anything that required memorization, like multiplication tables. I only learned my ABCs because of the "ABCDEF" song. That mnemonic would prove invaluable, for reasons unrelated to education, in my early twenties.

School was within two miles of our house, and as such there was no bus service. Mom could take us but we had to go in real early with her, and there was not a lot of fun in that. We rode our bikes to school as long as the weather wasn't frightful. Otherwise, Brian's or Steve's mom took turns, with Mom being the transportation choice of last resort. Georgia joined us on our morning daily commute. Afternoons she had cheerleader practice most days, and she got a ride home from one of the cool kids' moms. In spite of Georgia's higher social status, she "knew" us at school even though she did not eat at our table.

Albert and Hope struggled adjusting to our new schedule and began to dig holes in Mom's azalea beds and chew on anything left on the porch. Mom was not happy and had taken to chasing them with her broom and muttering what I expected were words from the forbidden list under her breath. On the whole, it looked more than a bit comical. We knew better than to laugh, though.

Albert sent me his slideshow pretty much every night, and I tried my best to send him one back cautioning him of the real and present danger of crossing Mom ... any further. It appeared this was a one-way radio channel. He did not get my message or chose to ignore it.

The school year flew by and before I knew it, it was Christmas break. South Georgia weather is pretty mild in December. Might have a few cold nights below freezing but they are pretty rare. That was a good thing this Christmas break. Albert signaled an emergency on the second night of break.

Georgia was at my window with Albert before my feet hit the ground. "Dad-gum Malvados," I mumbled.

It had rained a good bit and the window had swelled and was difficult to open. Georgia could not help because the screen blocked her. I got it open with an exaggerated grunt accompanied with an exceptionally loud and smelly fart in mixed company. I smothered my giggle as I heard footsteps coming down the hall. I shushed Georgia with my forefinger to my lips, dove back under the covers and feigned sleep. Mom peeked around the corner but did not enter the room. Mom stifled a cackle as she tiptoed down the hall back to her room. The rank smell of my fart explained the noise, giving cover to my attempted midnight breakout.

That was a good thing as my heart was racing faster than Richard Petty's Plymouth at Daytona. I would fold and confess at even the most cursory of interrogations and be in crazy trouble for attempting to sneak out of the house. I wasn't sure what the punishment might be, but I expected a fate worse than death—like an endless school year with mean ol' Miss Hawkins without recess. She was balding, had a wandering eye and a giant nose with a massive hairy wart at the end. Not really … she was an attractive twenty-something-year-old woman. We just drew her that way 'cause she yelled a lot and threw chalk board erasers at our heads. She had a pretty good aim for a southpaw. I expect her teaching career was cut short. Kids were not her jam.

After waiting a few minutes, I unfastened the screen and slid out the window, pulling it down behind me. Albert barked with urgency. The Malvados had captured another puppy. I still considered Albert a puppy but, truth be told, he was growing like a weed and weighed at least seventy pounds. He led the way to the Malvados' front yard.

There was no moon tonight and it was pitch dark. The only illumination was from the Christmas lights on about half the houses. Perversely, the Malvados had decorated their yard for the joyous holiday season. The yard was crisscrossed with thousands of red, blue, green and white twinkling lights. It looked like a sad used car lot where old junk cars made a final plea for a new home before making their journey to the scrap heap. The wind was up and the colored lights swayed, casting eerie shadows across the front lawn. Someone was sitting in a rocking chair on the front porch singing lewd versions of Christmas carols freakishly in an angelic voice.

Georgia looked at me. "Did he just say—"

I raised my eyebrows and nodded yes. "I think he might be drunk. Maybe he's the only one awake."

Carried by the breeze we could hear the faint pitiful whining of a puppy from around back. The hair stood up along Albert's spine. He emitted a low, ominous growl. His eyes narrowed and he pinned his ears back. Georgia grabbed his collar and tried to soothe him. We needed a plan.

The inside of the house was pitch black, but since outside it was brightly lit in disturbing holiday cheer, stealth would be challenging. Other than the obscene caroler, we saw no movement. We were still hiding behind the shell of a rusted-out '55 Bel Air when the caroler yelled, "Get off my darn lawn, you pesky trespassers." His language may have been a touch more colorful. I surveyed his lawn. Patches of gravel, weeds, broken-down cars and miscellaneous trash and clutter. I had yet to be formally introduced to the word irony, but I am pretty certain this was that.

I wasn't confident whether the lewd caroler had spotted us or was just yelling at random shadows of Christmas past or future. I made a mental note to never drink alcohol. Grands, I may have ignored some of the lessons of my childhood in my later years.

He cleared up my confusion in short order. "You snotty-nose little rich kids need to get off my lawn before I sic my dog on you."

Rich kids—well, that was something new. I guess that word, perspective, comes into play again. I realized the man on the porch wasn't a man at all but a kid in our class. He was a couple of years older than me but he was still a kid. Georgia turned to me and said, "That's Rusty."

I nodded my head yes. I stood up and called out, "Rusty," in a hushed tone so as not to alert any slumbering Malvados.

He squinted and shielded his eyes from the light. "Dog. That you, boy?"

I said, "Yes." Not the time nor place to make an issue of this intentional slight.

Georgia stood up and introduced herself. Of course, everyone knew Georgia. This should play in our favor as, after all, Rusty was a couple of years older and, as such, retained less natural protection from what Mom called female wiles. It is like one day girls have cooties and then the next you are slobbering all over yourself to carry their books, all for the benefit of a fleeting smile. Perhaps God has a wicked sense of humor and designed us with a set of amusing human frailties just for his entertainment. Preacher did routinely stress the vast length of eternity, and all that singing and praising got wicked boring for me after just a few minutes.

"What you doing on my lawn in the middle of the night, Dog?" Rusty yelled back, adding a couple of mocking barks. Funny thing is, bullies like Rusty can't hurt my feelings. I just don't care what they think or say about me. Only people I care about can hurt me. Sadly, they can hurt me a lot. I just hoped Rusty wasn't yelling and barking loud enough to wake any of his unruly kin.

"We've come to get the puppy." I decided just to play this straight. I kind of felt sorry for him. He came to school every day wearing dirty clothes and smelling. Most of the other kids made fun of him behind his back. Rusty was a big kid and older than us, so no one was dumb enough to cross him to his face. He ate his free school lunch alone, scowling at anyone that dared look his way. And like I said, this was an embarrassment at the time. Likely though, looking back, this was his only meal of the day. I don't think he was a bad kid. We just painted him that way and he accepted the role he was given.

"You ain't getting the dog. My uncle training him to be a fighting dog." Rusty stood up. He was a lot bigger than me and he had a baseball bat in his hand. Albert growled. "Stay back," Rusty warned, pointing the barrel of the bat at my head.

"Rusty," Georgia called out. "We are taking the dog. You gonna hit me with that bat?" She moved ahead of me toward him. I held Albert back. I really didn't think he had it in him to hit a girl. Me on the other hand …

Rusty raised the bat above his head. "I'm warning you."

Albert yanked hard, pulling me to the ground. This was likely gonna end poorly for someone. Georgia kept a slow, steady pace toward him. "Rusty, your uncle is passed out drunk inside. He will never know how the pup got away. Be a man, Rusty, and just let us take the dog."

"Stay back," he whimpered. His face grimaced like he was about to cry.

"Where did you get the puppy?" Georgia asked softly.

"Tyson Park. My brother jumped in the ditch and saved him after the mutt fell in during a thunderstorm."

"Well, that was heroic. Be sure and tell your brother thank you," Georgia noted the act heroic, not the brother a hero. Heroic acts can be performed for illicit motives, which kind of nullifies the hero label. Saving a dog from drowning just to subject him to a fate far worse is not the act of a hero.

We have confused and devalued the term hero, mistakenly calling victims and even just decent human acts heroic. A hero risks his or her own safety to assist a third party. In this case, a dog. For instance, even saving your own life is not an act of heroism. Escaping from a disaster, good on you—not heroic. The victim of a disaster is not a hero for merely saving themselves. It's a smart thing to do, perhaps even brave, just not heroic. Returning a lost billfold to its rightful owner or helping an old lady across the street is neither a brave nor a heroic act. Those are acts of human decency. Grands, at a minimum, be decent humans, but do not expect accolades and awards for just doing the right thing. In real life there are no participation trophies.

Georgia kept walking toward Rusty while motioning with her hand for me to go around. I was confused but Albert understood. He broke free from my grip and ran around to the back yard with his ears and tail pinned down. It was go time. I followed, trusting Georgia's instincts she could handle Rusty.

We found the puppy there lying in a pool of his own blood, whimpering, chained to the oak tree with the rusted-out engine. I was angry, very angry. Albert was as well. I unchained the dog but could barely carry him. He weighed at least fifty pounds. His face was smashed and was covered in blood. He licked my face. I started crying.

I wasn't sure he would live unless we got him to a vet, and even with my Christmas and birthday money I couldn't afford to pay a vet. But I could not let the dog die. It just wasn't right. I closed my eyes. "Jesus," I prayed, "it's high time you showed yourself."

My blood was up as I got back to the front of the house. I sat the dog down at Rusty's feet. "You see what you did," I yelled, forcing Rusty's head down to look at the carnage committed by his family.

Georgia shushed me. "Don't wake up the others."

I didn't care. I could take them all, I thought. I yanked the bat out of Rusty's hand and was about to swing it before Albert jumped on me, knocking me to the ground. Rusty started crying. I threw the bat down and picked up the puppy without effort. Maybe Jesus was listening and I was the one that wasn't. We walked straight back to the house. I dared any Malvado to mess with me tonight.

Mom met us at the back porch. "Where have you been, young man?" she scolded. "It's the middle of the—" First she saw the injured puppy, and then she saw my tear-soaked face.

Mom had some "rainy day money" saved up. She pooled her money with ours and we took the puppy to the vet later in the morning once he opened. The dog's jaw was broken. His left eye swollen shut. There were several cuts on his body and the vet said he likely had some broken ribs but couldn't tell for sure without an x-ray. He did not have an x-ray. We would have to drive the hour over to the animal hospital in Albany for that. People doctors did not have x-rays. He tried to pulled Mom aside. I knew what he was gonna say.

"We ain't putting him down, Doc. Doug will not abide." I had taken to talking in the third person when I wanted to be taken seriously by adults.

"It would be best, son. It's gonna cost a couple of hundred dollars at least to get him well and he will suffer … maybe even still not make it."

I did it. I said words that were on the top of the forbidden list. "Gosh-darn the Malvados." But I used the forbidden words on the very top of the list. Mom did not scold me. This was not an idle curse, so the Lord's name was not invoked in vain.

"Malvados did this?" the vet asked, shaking his head in disgust.

I nodded, holding back the tears. A boy was not supposed to cry and I had already more than exhausted my tear quota. Georgia was bawling, but she was a girl, after all.

The vet turned to Mom. "Been hearing some really bad stories about them Malvados supplying dogs for a dog-fighting ring up near Valdosta. You be careful, you hear. Big money in dog fighting and with big money comes big trouble." The vet turned to me and asked, "How much you got there, son?"

I counted out our pool of money from my pocket. "Twenty-seven dollars and thirty-two cents, an arrowhead, two paper clips..."—I paused and pulled off my prized necklace and added it to the pile— "and a priceless tiger shark tooth necklace."

"Twenty-seven dollars thirty-two cents and two paper clips should cover it. Leave him with me a few days. I'll get him better. Gosh-darn Malvados," the vet mumbled, repeating my curse.

The puppy lay on the table whimpering with a pleading eye. I gave him a hug, avoiding his clearly broken jaw. His face was grossly misshapen. One side did not match the other. It was asymmetrical. We tend to judge symmetry as beauty when both halves of something look alike. Some might say his face was the opposite of beauty, but that someone would be wholly mistaken. One eye was larger and set a bit higher on his face. The entirety of his jaw tilted right with his large canine tooth permanently protruding outside his jawline. He was a thing of beauty to me in spite of his filth, malnutrition and physical defects. That whole beauty lies within, Grands, it is a real thing. Little did I know at the time his soul was even more beautiful and he came with a special super power just like his brother Albert.

"His jaw going to heal like that?" I asked.

"I am afraid it is, son," the vet responded.

I looked the puppy into his good eye and gently stroked his head. "It's okay, Jaws. Everything is going to be all right."

Jaws lifted his head and wagged his tail.

CHAPTER EIGHT

Mom drove us from the vet in silence to Royal's Drug Store downtown just across the street from the First Bank of Tifton. There were a lot of "Firsts" in Tifton and a handful of "Seconds," mostly churches. Not many "Thirds," though. It was a small town.

Brian's mom worked at the soda counter inside the drugstore where you could get short order food. They were known for their grilled cheese sandwiches, sodas and ice cream. You could pay for stuff on account. I once asked Dad what on account meant. He said, "It's on account you ain't got any money." Mom had spent our last dime at the vet. This purchase would be on account.

Clerks at a drugstore soda fountain were, for a reason beyond my understanding, called soda jerks. I could not call Miss Nancy a jerk of any sort or risk getting my mouth washed out with soap. And, Grands, this was a literal, physical threat. Jerk was on the forbidden list of words. She was wearing uncharacteristically heavy makeup, but there was no denying Miss Nancy had a shiner. Her eye was black, blue and several indeterminate shades of yellow, and was unmistakably swollen.

"You fall down?" I asked. Mom shushed me. I knew she had not fallen. I was turning eleven in a few days. I had grown up a lot over the summer. I knew what was what.

Miss Nancy, Brian's mom, forced a smile as we sat on the cracked leather stools at the counter. "What you having?" She obsessively wiped the spotless marble countertop down with a rag.

Mom replied, "Two grilled cheese sandwiches and two cokes with one side of french-fried potatoes." The cultural contribution of the French was a mystery to me but I knew they had nailed the recipe for frying potatoes in animal fat, and for that I would be forever grateful to the French and salute their haughty cuisine. To this day I celebrate Bastille Day solely on account of french fries. I protested the single order, though. Me and my tummy monster liked french fries, a lot, and did not want to share the single order with Georgia.

"You can share," Mom said. It was years later I noticed this was not an uncommon theme. Mom would take us places and not get anything for herself. It wasn't like she wasn't hungry. I was too self-absorbed to notice her sacrifice.

Miss Nancy added a large spoonful of butter into the cast iron frying pan sitting on the hot plate and laid four slices of white bread within. The frozen potatoes sizzled, sending tiny scorching hot aromatic droplets of grease into the air as she dropped the starchy delicacies into the fryer. A puddle of drool formed on the countertop at my stool.

Miss Nancy poured us three cokes from the stainless-steel fountain into elegantly curved glasses filled with crushed ice and displaying a Pepsi logo. In the South, coke was generic for cola. Mom shook her head and held up two fingers. Miss Nancy smiled and pushed all three sodas to us. Mom did not touch hers. She had taken charity from the vet. Our twenty-seven dollars and thirty-two cents and two paper clips would not begin to cover the vet bill. She was at her charitable limit. We quickly drained our cokes and Miss Nancy refilled them with a sly wink. We were sitting in high cotton.

When the order was ready, Mom moved us over to the only booth in the store. This might be my last meal, I thought. I scarfed down two-thirds of the french fries with a half bottle of catsup before I touched my sandwich. Mom had said share, but nothing about equally.

Georgia frowned. "You eat like a pig." She meant it as an insult but it wasn't.

I knew I was fixin' to get the "I am disappointed in you, young man" and/or the "don't make me tell your father" talk. I had already formulated a plan to negotiate for the more desirable switch.

Grands, I'll save you the entire lecture and summarize. Mom came up with this new punishment that had never even been heard of. I was grounded for sneaking out of the house. She must have read about "grounding" in a Ladies Home Journal or Southern Living at one of her rare trips to the beauty shop. Mom went on to list the terms. No TV. I rarely watched TV except for Saturday morning cartoons and the occasional war movie. Okay ... maybe more than occasional. No phone. Was this a joke? I only picked up our phone because Dad yelled at me to answer the phone.

I was hoping she would ground me from vegetables, daily baths and dental hygiene as well. She did not. She continued her ground rules, adding no friends over inside the house. I covertly noted she said inside, not under the house or in the yard. This was a loophole I planned to exploit. My cardboard fort was adjacent to the oil-burning furnace. It stayed warm even on the coldest day. Now that I am writing this, I am pretty certain my fort was a serious fire hazard. We were home by ourselves during the day and whatever restriction she might want to impose would be difficult to enforce. She made me swear on an imaginary stack of Bibles I would never ever sneak out again at night. I did, and I meant to keep my promise. But sometimes a kid has to do what a kid has to do.

∞∞∞∞

Christmas Eve was our big family night. My dad's mother, his siblings and their extended families came to our house to exchange presents and have, by any comparison, a feast. Dad splurged and let Mom bake a giant precooked store-bought ham. A ham was pork. Those store cooks always left the meat a touch raw for Mom's taste. She cooked the flavor out of all meat, but pork she took to a different level. You could get worms from undercooked pork, Mom swore. She was right about the worms.

The other families brought over their specialty dishes to share. Granny always brought chicken dumplings made from scratch. These were by all accounts amazing and rarely lasted for seconds. Granny said the secret was selecting a fat hen. At one point this meant selecting a hen scurrying around her back yard and wringing its neck. Mom called this pot-luck dinner. I am not sure where the luck was in it nor why she elevated this meal from supper to lofty dinner status, unless supper was a small evening meal while dinner was a feast.

Mom baked the ham in the early afternoon and set it out on the kitchen table to cool. Dad just worked half days on Christmas Eve and would cut and carve the ham after washing up from work. Mom served the ham at room temperature. Worms were to be feared but bacteria were not a concern. And here Mom was wrong. Freshly baked ham produces a powerfully tantalizing aroma to a human, but to a growing puppy, all sense of caution would be at risk in order to locate, secure and consume the delicacy.

Jaws was just a few days home from the vet and still recovering from malnutrition as well as a multitude of injuries. He spent his nights with Georgia and Albert and days mostly wandering around in our back yard supervising Albert and Hope in the evisceration of Mom's azaleas. It was clear that Jaws, in spite of just returning to the pack and his physical disability, was the growing pack's alpha. He still moved slowly with a limp. One eye remained swollen shut and he oozed a malodorous gunk from a couple of wounds but otherwise seemed to be getting on okay.

Perspective. I tell you, it means a lot and is an important concept to grasp. It's hard to empathize with another's plight in life if you don't understand they may rightfully see the same event a tad differently.

It reminds me of a story our preacher used to tell, although the way he told it kind of bothered me. Preacher was a self-educated man who possessed only a marginal grip of the knowledge and wisdom contained in the ancient text of the King James version of the Holy

Bible. What he lacked in knowledge he made up for in passion and storytelling ability. He would make a great liar. Some said he was. Anyways, best not go down that rabbit hole.

At church one day, Preacher had told us the first-hand story of a man he personally knew who was without shoes. The man, you see, was busy complaining to Preacher regarding his lack of footwear, when they came upon a man with no feet. The moral, Preacher pointed out, is there's always someone worse off than yourself.

Me, knowing Preacher had several pairs of perfectly good shoes, wondered why he, being a godly man, did not give the shoeless man a pair. I doubted the job of preacher at our Missionary Baptist country church paid much, but he lived in the church-owned house with free utilities. And the man rarely bought a meal. All the church wives vied to have Preacher and his blue-haired, Amway-hawking wife over for dinner or, better still, the highly coveted Sunday lunch slot.

I asked Dad about Preacher's spare shoes. He said I missed the point of the story. I did not really think I did. I was a kid. but I got that it was a parable of sorts about perspective. Later I learned apparently a lot of other preachers personally knew the very same shoeless and footless men. Go figure. Those two fellows sure got around a lot, given their mobility challenges. And I knew no one, at least at the time, could give a man new feet, but why did none of these self-righteous storytellers not give the other man a pair of their old shoes?

I think Dad and Preacher missed the important point. Just 'cause you can't save the whole world doesn't mean you can't make a difference in a handful of people's or critters' lives.

So, getting back to that Christmas dinner … as Mom would often say and rarely do, long story short, Jaws, relatively speaking, was doing okay. For sure his appetite was ravenous. One of my chores was taking out the garbage to the outside bin. I argued, unsuccessfully, that was an inside chore and therefore in the purview of my sister's obligations.

That afternoon, I propped the screen door open with the rubber wedge placed there for that purpose. Jaws, possessed by the monster in his belly, seized the opening, leapt through the breach snagging the ham in his mangled jaws, and dashed under the house with remarkable agility. Mom stood speechless, her mouth agape in horror.

My survival instinct kicked in. I ran for the hills. Since there were no mountains in south Georgia, I ran to my secret fire-hazard fort underneath the house and watched my pack devour the Christmas ham with not a bit of concern to the coming consequences.

I had to come inside at some point and knew what would be waiting. Mom was angry as well, after her azaleas had been torn to shreds and now her overcooked ham defiled by the pack. She had precious little patience left for the puppies. I would have no allies in this battle. The Christmas Eve Ham incident, as it would be known to be called in the annals of Tifton history, pushed her over her level of tolerance for the pack's destructive shenanigans. Seemed a bit unfair that I carried the entire weight of the blame on my narrow shoulders, but somebody had to pay for that ham and that somebody's name was Doug.

Dad was waiting for me at the kitchen table with a glass of iced sweet tea in front of him and his belt slung from the back of my chair. He looked up from the evening paper when he heard me come in. "Bring me my belt." It was part of his theater. It was an especially brutal spanking. Usually Dad stopped when I started bawling, but I had vowed not to cry and I fully intended to keep that promise at any cost. Truth be told, my eyes leaked a bit, but I did not make a sound nor did I reach up to wipe the tears from my face. Eventually Mom stepped in after my sister started sobbing and shaking hysterically.

"You'll ruin Christmas," Mom cautioned. That train had left the station, I thought. I walked deliberately to my room where I quietly pushed the door closed and wept silently into my pillow stroking the tooth from the long-ago dead tiger shark. I prayed to God, "If you are there it is about time you showed yourself, Mister." I had just as well have prayed to the ancient shark.

Sue brought me a pillow to sit on but I shunned her gesture. I wasn't giving Dad the satisfaction. I was late to get in line for dinner and Granny's dumplings were all gone. Without the ham or dumplings, I was forced to eat a lot of unsavory vegetables to satisfy the monster within. After dinner, I went to the dessert table and picked out a generous slice of warm pecan pie, and added a giant serving spoon of vanilla ice cream. It was my favorite.

Dad snatched the pie from my hands. "You won't be having dessert tonight, son." In that moment, that whole honor-thy-father commandment was the toughest one on Moses' rocky shall list.

After everyone finished dinner and the ladies cleaned up, we exchanged gifts. Like I said, girls got the short end of the stick. We were all poor. My uncle L.A. worked at a bank and dressed up every day for work, but they were poor as well. The gifts were mostly from the need, not want, list. Underwear, shoes, socks, britches, school supplies ... none of us minded. This is what we knew.

My grandmother on my mom's side was a whole other level below poor. At her house, they had just recently gotten electricity. A single naked light bulb proudly hung in the center of their one-room house. The bulb was revered no less than a World Series trophy would someday be for the Braves. Inside plumbing was still a few years away. They drew their drinking water from a mechanical cast-iron-pump deep well on the back porch and their bathing and cooking water from a shallow bucket well located dangerously adjacent to the outhouse. Even at ten, I found the co-location of potable water to an open sewer absurd.

Grandma wasn't there. They didn't own a car and she wasn't that sociable anyway. But we opened her gifts on Christmas Eve. She was a mean old woman and, given perspective, I understand that now. To Grandma, life was simple. You are born. You suffer. You die.

Grandma never learned to spell my name. Doug—how hard is that, I thought. Curiously she was inconsistent even in the misspelling of my name. "Dug," which I kind of get because that is how it sounds. "Dough," an entirely different word. "Douge," a nonsensical yet favored frequent misspelling. My least beloved misspelling, though, was Dog. Like I said, it is the people I loved who could hurt me, sometimes without even knowing it. Tonight, Grandma had addressed my Christmas present, "To Dog."

Sue had already opened her present from Grandma: a bath towel. I got a similar mismatched towel. Tifton boasted a large cotton mill. The mill had a store that sold seconds, defective products, at a discount. Not complaining about the present. I was grateful she remembered me, her firstborn grandson, at all. Mom and Dad got a single towel to share between them. Grandma was not keen on the man who stole her eldest—and surrogate mom to the bottom half of the lineup—away at only sixteen. Mom was the oldest of nine siblings. Baseball, it seemed, was in my very DNA.

Christmas morning, Santa would bring us some more of the same from the need list, but the jolly fat bearded fellow always included a bit of loose change, unshelled pecans, a pear, maybe a fig or two, and one gift from the want list. A toy of some kind, a baseball, sometimes two, or a new mitt. In spite of my sore behind and missed dessert, it was a great night. I enjoyed my family and cherished the time I spent with them. But it was time for everyone to pack up their booty and leave. The quicker we got to bed, the sooner Santa and his improbable flying reindeers could make their epic journey and I could open the one gift that made Christmas special. Sorry, baby Jesus, but I was just a kid and it was the single present I looked forward to opening the entire year.

Between the excitement, a belly stuffed with bacon-grease-seasoned vegetables, and the butt pain, I had trouble falling asleep. I thought I heard Santa in the living room, but I dared not inspect. I had questioned Mom about Santa now for a couple of years. She implied Santa was real as long as I believed he was real. That created a bit of a dilemma. The physics of a flying sleigh circumnavigating the world overnight seemed improbable at best. And we, along with most in our neighborhood, did not have a chimney. Nevertheless, for selfish reasons alone, I erred on the side of belief.

A ruler, compass and protractor along with more clothes, undergarments and socks lay under the Christmas tree. Dad sipped coffee on the plastic-covered sofa in the living room. I couldn't look at him. I tore into my one wrapped present. It was small but heavy. The wrapped present was always the gift from our want list. I had circled and dog-eared the pages for several suggested items from the Sears Roebuck toy catalog. My parents unmistakably knew what I wanted, and I knew at best I would get one item from the toy catalog. Even so I was grateful for the gift. We were poor; this is what I knew.

The outside of the box said it was a King James Bible … a Scofield edition. I wasn't worried. Mom repurposed boxes for this very reason and I knew Dad coveted a Scofield Bible. It was a reference Bible like the preachers used. My real Christmas gift was hidden inside the box for Dad's new Bible. I tore the box open to find a brand-new Scofield King James Bible embossed in gold lettering with my given name: Dog.

My dad looked hard at me with his good eye waiting for complaint. My fanny was in no condition to take another beating so I bit my tongue. "See there, son," Dad said, pointing at the misspelling of my name. "Santa got it embossed special just for you."

My Santa dilemma was forever resolved.

CHAPTER NINE

My fur crew kept smartly out of sight for the next few months. School flew by, and at home I had followed the lead of the dogs and avoided my parents. I barely spoke a word to them. Dad didn't seem to notice, but I could tell Mom was starting to get concerned. I was not a sullen kid. Didn't help much that Mom was still mad at the dogs. Between school and it getting dark so early, I had very little time with the pack, except on weekends.

Georgia's dad liked the dogs and she did not have to hide them. I missed them but visited them at Georgia's as often as I could. Her dad liked the pups—me not so much. He had taken to asking me my intentions with his daughter. Wasn't sure what that meant but Georgia always blushed. I looked up "intentions" in the Webster. "Purpose in respect to marriage." Now, I was even more confused. Marriage was for old people. I was a kid, still thoughtfully debating the cootie coefficient of the female gender.

Come March, we started playing baseball again. The dogs joined us. The additional year of growth proved too much for Tyson Park. In spite of our ground rules, we were launching balls out of the park left and right and losing them with great regularity. We tried to train the dogs to retrieve the balls, but it proved futile at best. Jaws would, if convenient, grab the ball in his grossly misshapen jaw but then he wanted to play tug of war with it. Despite his injuries at the hand of humans, he was a lovable dog. Trusting, not so much. He would emit a low growl and assume a defensive posture any time a stranger approached us.

Jaws' tug of war was not good for the health and well-being of baseballs. Many a day we ended the game playing an inning or two with a pine cone, a wad of duct tape or an imaginary ball. Albert and Hope liked to run the bases with us. They were not keen on the rules but had a blast. Hope liked getting in a pickle, but when she ran out of the baseline Brian was quick to call her out. His own dog, for goodness sake. Jaws planted himself on home plate and surveyed the madness making the occasional editorial comment from his throne. We needed a new, more sustainable solution.

Across the street from our house was an empty lot. Actually, it was three lots, but it was overgrown. Georgia's uncle had a farm and knew the owner of the lot. He brought over a farm tractor with a bush hog and cut the brush, scrub oaks and weeds down to a manageable height. The neighborhood kids banded together with shovels, rakes, picks, saws, hatchets and push mowers. With Brian's careful supervision we carved out a respectable baseball diamond over a period of a couple of weeks.

Georgia was the only girl who rolled up her sleeves and helped us, but an entire gaggle of neighborhood girls turned out to watch us work. They sipped lemonade and giggled at our exploits, sitting on a blanket spread out in the shade of a mimosa tree. The girls were soon covered in little pink puff-balls from the tree's flowers. The older boys took to taking long breaks on the blanket picking the mimosa blooms from the girls' hair. Georgia squashed my protest, telling me to "give it a rest."

Home plate was up against a little rise with a plum tree partially shielding the neighbor's windows from errant balls. The outfield butted up against a deep ditch, but it took a real hit to reach it. It would last us a couple years before we outgrew this field as well.

Every action, no matter how well intended, has an unexpected and often negative consequence. Your physics teacher will later explain this as "every action has an equal and opposite reaction." I have always found the reactions much less predictable than merely equal and opposite. The field-clearing displaced an assortment of local wildlife, most notably my nemesis, the water moccasin. Most snakes, even the poisonous variety, mind their own business and are no real danger to humans unless humans get stupid. Alas, it is the nature of us humans to get stupid. Poke a rattlesnake with a short stick and suffer the rather unpleasant consequences.

But water moccasins are mean and aggressive and will fearlessly attack without provocation. Fat and gray, they are poisonous but usually not deadly. Still, they were known to chase a full-grown man across a pond, jump in his boat and gnaw his leg off for no particular reason other than 'cause they were ornery critters. I expected some of them were big enough they could eat a toddler. I was wrong about all this, but still I was deathly scared of water moccasins. I had inherited this fear, according to my mom, and I passed it on to my namesake in spades. Sorry, Doug Junior. Even sorrier, Megan. Mom, in fact, was scared of all reptiles, including lizards, turtles and even frogs, real, stuffed, cast or animated.

Mom smiled and waved from across the street. She was making a show at sweeping the front porch in order to keep a distant eye on us. It was bottom of the sixth and two out again. Kenny, a fast runner, was on second and the game was tied according to the pebble pile, eleven to eleven. We had taken to using pebbles to keep score as Brian had a way of manipulating scores to his team's benefit. Brian, for the record, became a highly successful tax accountant as an adult. Grands, you will get that comment later when rereading this book to my great-grandchildren.

Steve was on the mound again. He got me last time, in a similar situation, with a change up to hit a home run out of the park, which at Tyson was sadly a ground rule out. But at the Lot, a home run, even in the ditch, was a home run. No one had yet earned that honor—at least not a home run out of the park. Brian was in deep center field almost to the ditch. Albert was on first. He liked running the bases. Hope was sitting with the girls under the mimosa, with a pink ribbon affixed to her collar and mimosa blooms in her fur. Jaws was halfway between our front porch and home plate, lounging in the shade of a scrub oak, visibly rolling his eyes and huffing at Hope. He sensed it was almost dinner time. Jaws was strongly opposed to all frivolity, unnecessary exercise and skipping a meal.

I had one strike and, like before, it did not matter how many balls because there were no walks. Steve did his elaborate wind-up. I knew a changeup was coming. It was high and outside and I laid off the ball. Brian from deep center field called a strike. Steve on the mound stayed silent, locked in the zone, determined to strike me out or force a lazy fly ball. Ground balls could be tricky given the irregular surface of the Lot. We took our baseball with more seriousness than it likely deserved.

Kenny turned and yelled to Brian, "Are you blind?"

Brian unconsciously pushed his thick glasses up the bridge of his nose. They were still held together with Scotch tape. I tried to like the boy but sometimes he could test the goodness of baby Jesus himself.

Steve wound up to throw again just as Mom let loose a bloodcurdling scream. I sprinted over to the house, bat in hand. Jaws beat me there. In his crooked mouth, he held the bottom three-quarters of a writhing water moccasin.

I heard Brian, nearly out of breath, running up from behind. "Calling strike three on that, Dog. We win."

Like I said, Brian was a hard boy to like. I bashed the still-gaping snake's mouth with the bat in my hand.

That night Mom hand-fed Jaws from the kitchen table. Dad objected but for once in her life she stood up to him. Jaws slept in my room that evening. Mom drew the line at the bed. I shared a blanket with him on the floor that night and pretty much every night thereafter until I graduated from high school. My darkness lifted. I was a whole boy again.

CHAPTER TEN

The mosquito has on occasion been called the state bird of Georgia. I believe this to be biting sarcasm. After an especially rainy spring, the flying dive bomber's population had increased to swarm levels often darkening the sky at dusk. We humans may have owned the day but the mosquitos owned the night. The state declared an emergency and funded a multi-pronged attack on the evil critters. Part of the assault was nightly fogging. Right about dusk every night the mosquito fogger came through our neighborhood spraying a chemical called DDT.

The chemical was excellent at killing mosquitos. The unintended consequence was the chemical was later proven pretty dadgum efficient at killing us humans and every other living organism on the planet. Just took a wee bit more time. We did not know this. Like I said, equal and somewhat opposite. It was an early lesson in man's hubris. We humans are self-assured of our mastery of science, but our certainties are frequently proven mistaken with time. Once upon a time it was settled by science the earth is flat. I hear it ain't.

We all pedaled our bikes to the top of the hill to meet the truck. Well, the boys did. The girls, I thought, were chicken. With perspective, I think the girls were just smarter than us. Some days there were as many as two dozen of us staged waiting for the fogger to make the right-hand turn down the hill. The furry pack smartly waited at the bottom of the hill, vigorously cheering us on, but from a safe distance. Occasionally, in their excitement, they would fight each other like a bunch of soccer hooligans.

The object of our endeavor was to see who could stay with the truck in the thick of the toxic fog the longest through our neighborhood. The fogger rarely exceeded twenty miles an hour, and going downhill it was easy to stay in the slipstream, blinded by the dense fog. On so many levels this was crazy dangerous, flying blind down the hill, sucking in the noxious fumes, mere inches from a moving truck. Even so it was a blast. More fun for me because I had amazing lung capacity and frequently won the contest. We will see how that plays out for your Papi in the long run. Sometimes what feels like a victory ... ain't.

Today was like most others. We paused our baseball game when we heard the distant sound of the fogger and grabbed our bikes to race up the hill to meet him. But today, unlike all others, Rusty was at the top of the hill waiting. Rusty's mount was a yellow spray-painted Schwinn. None of the kids in our neighborhood could afford a Schwinn, and I could think of but one reason someone would ruin the paint job of the bike. The

Schwinn was, as Mom liked to say, "ill gotten." I later learned the term for this is *euphemism*. It is a nice way of saying something bad like "stolen."

At school I gave Rusty a wide berth. We had not spoken since we rescued Jaws. He nodded. "How's my dogs?" He had "up to no good" in his eyes.

"Not your dogs." He was bigger than me and could likely take me but I was scared of no one. Snakes, the dark, steamed vegetables, the boogie man ... yes, but not any kids. I could hold my own in a scrap and ain't no one gonna take my dogs away.

Brian was bigger than me and was full of false bluster, but he was scared of Rusty. Brian pretty much was scared of his own shadow. Steve and Kenny were older, but thanks to a recent growth spurt I was bigger than them both by a wide margin. Besides, it was my dog, my fight. There is no backing down from a bully, and your mom, as much as she may desire, can't magically protect you from every threat. Rusty might best me, but he would know he had been in a scrap. It was one of the good lessons Dad taught me. Never start a fight but don't run from one either. And once a fight starts, fight to win.

Now, Grands, Papi is not advocating violence as a solution to settling disputes. In fact, I am strongly against using violence to resolve said differences. What I am saying is that there are some bad people in the world that the only thing they understand is force. And most of these bad people expect you to be passive, to do nothing, but take whatever they dish out. Bullies depend upon your passivity. Once you let the bullies know you will not stand silent, they will likely leave you alone to go and find a more malleable target.

The very best armor against bullies is yourself. Mom, the teacher or the police will not always be at your side. Learn self-reliance. Learn your own self-worth. If someone calls you a "fat head," it doesn't change the size or shape of your head. If your head is fat, own it. If it's not, laugh. Either way, always try to walk away from a quarrel with your head held high. The opinions and insults of strangers or casual acquaintances should remain irrelevant, unimportant to you and incapable of hurting your feelings as you just don't care.

Speak softly in disagreement and be slow to anger. Never is it okay to meet an insult with a fist or injure an innocent party. Be prepared to help others that are incapable of helping themselves. And furthermore, do not be a bully. Never take advantage of someone or something weaker than you just because you can. Bullies are vile and despicable creatures. Papi and Grinnie do not abide bullies.

We had taken to attaching a handful of baseball cards, using a wooden clothespin fastened by rubber bands to the fork of our bikes. The cards were positioned in a manner to strike the wheel's spokes as they spun, simulating a motor sound. As well as making the cool sound, it helped us find each other in the thick fog and avoid collisions. I pulled my cards back out of the spokes. I needed stealth.

We suspiciously eyed each other, Rusty and I, as the fogger approached, poised to sprint down the hill once the truck made its turn. The fogger driver shook his head, chuckled silently and waved but as usual made no attempt to stop us. Boys will be boys. It was a common mantra. Rusty reached out and kicked my bike, knocking me to the pavement as I politely waved back to the driver. Rusty sprinted down the hill inches from the fogger. I got up and stomped on the bike's pedals, giving enthusiastic chase as if my young life depended on it. I passed the other kids within the first twenty yards as they lay back, rightfully expecting trouble.

Close to the bottom of the hill I could hear the dogs barking and made out Rusty just a couple of feet ahead of me. He looked back, silhouetted in the fog, and grinned. I pulled alongside as he produced a short stick. I shrugged and started to pull away as he jammed the stick into the front spokes of my bike. I tumbled head over heels over the handlebars as the bike came to an abrupt stop. Brian and Steve narrowly missed me. Kenny flew by bravely giving chase to Rusty.

Jaws came up to me and licked my bleeding forehead and sniffed the raspberry that extended the entirety of both my legs. Seeing I would likely survive and had not spilled food from my pockets, Jaws sprinted after Rusty, his ears and tail pinned. I yelled, "No." I wiped the blood-tinged sweat out of my eyes and jumped on my bike, but the wheel was bent and could not pass through the fork. I snatched Brian's bike and took off in the direction of Rusty and Jaws.

By the time I caught up, Jaws had yanked Rusty off his bike to the pavement. Albert had passed me en route and was tearing at Rusty's pants leg. I grabbed Jaws. Georgia came from nowhere and pulled Albert away, kicking Rusty in the ribs for good measure. We walked back home in silence. Rusty wasn't hurt bad but the fogger driver had witnessed our dogs yanking him off the bike. He had stopped his truck and did not drive away until Rusty got up and slithered away with his ill-gotten Schwinn. Out of context it appeared our dogs were aggressive, not protective. We were both worried about the consequences.

Said consequences were not long in coming. Next morning the dog-catcher, what you Grands would now call Animal Control, was knocking on our door. Mom and Dad had left for work. School was out but Mom had gotten a part-time job spelling Shirley at Dalton's. Sue as usual was in her room. It was fairly uncommon in the day to keep dogs inside. I shushed Jaws and for once he minded. I answered the door.

"Your mom home, son?" the officer asked. He was in a forest green uniform with a shiny badge. On his belt, he had pepper spray, handcuffs and a nightstick. Still I kept the screen door fastened.

"No, sir," I answered honestly.

"You home by yourself?"

"No, sir." I made a real effort not to lie but saw no reason to volunteer information. And no kid was a fan of the town's dog-catcher. Seemed like a horrible profession somewhere close to the bottom of the list of honorable employment along with lawyers, politicians and other no-good degenerates.

"Can I talk to your caretaker?" the dog-catcher asked.

"Huh?" I should have said sir but, like I said, not a fan. I wasn't clear as to the meaning of caretaker. One who takes care?

"Who is watching you, son?" he asked, puzzled. Surely, he must have thought, this eleven-year-kid is not at home alone.

"Oh. you mean my much, much older sister?" Not that she watched me but she was at home and technically in charge of my well-being.

I ran down the hall and got Sue. She would have no clue what happened but knew Jaws stayed in the house. Sue ordinarily pretended I did not exist and I happily returned the favor. She was four years older and wanted to have nothing to do with her bratty, snot-nosed, fart machine of a brother. Her words, not mine—true that they were.

The truth is almost always the best option, and, Grands, let me encourage you to stick to the truth. But for the life of me on this day I could not see a path out of this mess with the truth and I needed Sue to tell a doozy. I expected her to relish the opportunity to throw me under the bus. She did not.

"Hello, Officer. How can I help you?"

"Do you own a large black dog, with a ..."—he referred to his notes—"a seriously jacked-up face?"

Sue looked at me for a minute. "Bless your heart," Sue replied. I was aghast. Bless your heart in Southern-speak was a strong insult, smothered and covered in kind words and a smile. "We don't own any dog."

She unceremoniously shut the door in the officer's face. He knocked again. Sue yelled through the shut door, "Go away or I will call the police. You are harassing little kids."

He dutifully left. I looked at Sue. "You did that for me?"

She shrugged. "We don't own a dog. We have a furry brother."

Maybe my sister was not my enemy after all. A couple of years later for sure we became allies against a common enemy, Dad. But in that moment for certain, I could not have loved her more.

CHAPTER ELEVEN

In the summer, it was difficult to keep track of days of the week. Monday felt like Tuesday ... Tuesday like Wednesday. The smell of pot roast slow-cooking in the crock pot with fresh potatoes and carrots signaled it was Sunday. Mom had yet to call me for breakfast, but I got up off the floor anyway to take Jaws out.

I nudged the hairy beast. He partially opened a solitary eye and low-growled at me. Jaws was spoiled beyond rotten. In the summer, he slept in till I was done with chores, except on Sundays, when I had to get him out of the house as Dad would be home all day. Jaws could smell the roast slow-cooking as well. He knew what was what and did not want to be evicted from his cozy spot.

I nudged him again. He jumped up from his growing pool of drool, barked and bit me playfully on the bum.

I heard Dad in the dining room. "What's that dog still doing in my house?" The power dynamic of the house had shifted to Mom. Dad had yet to fully accept the shift.

I rolled my eyes and led Jaws, drooling from the smell of the pot roast, down the hall and out the back door. Mom had already placed a bowl of milk, the end pieces from a loaf of bread and some day-old scrambled eggs out for him. Jaws was, despite the ham, her hero. She would never forget that Jaws had risked his life in order to save hers.

After breakfast, I got dressed for church. I did not mind Sunday School so much. I had a different set of friends at church, and Dalton was our teacher. For a butcher, he was a kind-hearted man, soft-spoken with a quick smile. He taught us Bible stories from the official Southern Baptist sanctioned lesson plan, but he was engaging and open to getting off subject.

Tifton is about 180 miles due south on what is now I-75. Just up that partially completed interstate was the greatest city in the South, Atlanta. And Atlanta was home to The Braves.

Now as far as Major League baseball teams were concerned, the Braves were gosh-awful, always last or close to last in the standings. I had seen them on TV only a couple of times. The Yankees, Dodgers and Red Sox were the only teams regularly televised. Saturday afternoon was the only time baseball was on TV until the playoffs and Series, and for sure the Braves had packed their ceremonial teepees and tomahawks by then. This was before ESPN was even thought of, and ESPN was decades before the birth of the regional sports channels that ensure almost every single baseball game is televised.

But there was something special about this team. They had a catcher named Joe Torre, who was a pretty good hitter that everyone talked about. Later in his career Torre successfully managed the Braves, Dodgers and even the Yankees. But the star of the team was a colored fellow named Hank Aaron.

Your mother just gasped, I am sure. Papi said "colored." Oh, no! Yes, I did. Today that term may be considered derogatory. But in this day, it was a polite term for Negro. Oh, no, Papi said "Negro." Grands, the term African-American wasn't created until way after Papi was a full-grown man. And no one used the term "Black" either. There was nothing hateful about the word colored. In fact, every kid I knew adored Hank Aaron. He was our hero. That said, in your world both of those terms are frowned upon. I get that, and you should respect that as well. Respect others even if they don't share the same point of view, religion, sex or skin color. Learn to judge individuals by their actions, not by their physical differences or similarities to you. Now Papi—you can call me any name that you want. A rose is, after all, a rose by any other name. At least that is what Bill Shakespeare said. I am who I am regardless of the series of ordered letters someone puts together to label me.

Hammerin' Hank was chasing the Babe's career home run record of 714. Later in life I was told that all us Southern Crackers were rooting against him on account of he was colored. I expect there were those that did, but I never personally met one of them. Even Dad was cheering for Hank, and Dad was the Webster definition of Cracker. There was even a picture of Dad, not smiling, included in the dictionary beside the definition of Cracker. I expect some Southern whites hated Hank—beats me—but for sure we were not among those. To say otherwise is rewriting history to fit a popular narrative and is just a bald-faced lie. We were color-blind and just wanted our hero Hank to take the record. That said, Hank related that he had received thousands of hate letters amongst his voluminous fan mail just 'cause he was colored. And for that, Mr. Aaron, I am truly sorry.

Just about everyone with a pulse was glued to the transistor radio every time Hank approached a milestone. A couple of years later, Hank hit 710 and all the TV networks covered his at-bats, interrupting all broadcasts, even the "Wonderful World of Disney." They even disrupted Yankees' game to show Hank bat. Once Hank topped Mickey Mantle, it was a magical thing to watch, and it was all we could talk about this Sunday in Sunday School. Dalton was excited too. We all could not wait until Hammerin' Hank of our very own Atlanta Braves shattered Babe's record.

Preacher, on the other hand, was oblivious to Hank's spiritual quest. He wasn't much of a sports fan at all. Preacher did not even fish or hunt and, for these parts, that was in itself suspicious behavior. Preacher also was unfamiliar with the world-famous NASCAR driver Richard Petty. To me it was a real head-scratcher how Preacher did not get rode out of town for being a Commie spy. This was the height of the Cold War and that was a thing.

We played paper football on the pine pews to pass the time as Preacher droned on well past the noon hour. He felt he did God a disservice if he didn't bore each and every one of us out of our wits on Sunday. I looked at Dad's watch and heavy sighed. It was twelve-thirty, and Preacher had yet to call for the invitation.

Like baseball, I had come to learn that God kept stats on preachers similar to wins and losses, strike-outs and walks. But God kept score based on attendance, cash offerings and souls saved. There was a literal scoreboard in the sanctuary posting these stats. I expect Preacher, like the Braves, was in God's cellar. We were a dirt-poor congregation, mostly row farmers who scratched out a meager living dependent on the unseen forces that dictated the weather and crop prices. The collection plate rarely filled with more than a few crumpled-up singles, pocket change, paper clips, plastic army men, breath mints, chewed gum, toothpicks and pocket lint. On occasion, I speculated some of the items left in the collection plate to be subtle editorial comments on Preacher's sermons.

For certain his sermons fell well short of inspirational or even lucid to the most faithful. The services were lightly attended. Consequently, Preacher tried a little too hard to make up for his otherwise pathetic stats on souls saved, threatening eternal H-E-double-hockey-sticks fire and brimstone in order to encourage the less faithful off the fence and into the fold. Think of Preacher as the number eight batter that always swung for the fences but struck out in spectacular fashion more often than not. And be reminded, in this day, the pitcher batted ninth even in the American League.

Finally, I thought, the portly windbag called for the invitation. "Hymnal number 323, Are You Washed in the Blood?" Us Christians admittedly got some freaky rituals for sure. Eating flesh and bathing in blood, high on that list. "Please stand."

Now there were only four verses of the song in the hymnal, but after all four were sung, not a single soul had walked down the crimson-red carpeted aisle to salvation. Not even one to rededicate their life to the Lord Jesus. Preacher wasn't having this. He held his Bible high in the air and called for a do-over. We started from verse one and after three more go-arounds inquiring into our bloody bathing tendencies, not soul one was saved. Goose eggs on the scoreboard all around. The Bible grew heavy and Preacher lowered his outstretched arm to a less celestial altitude. He moved to plan B, calling on deacons down to pray at the "Altar of Christ." Some lay flat on their bellies. I expect this was because the tile floor was uncomfortable on the knees during an anticipated extended prayer session. This was not their first rodeo.

Georgia looked back at me and rolled her eyes. I motioned for her, wiggling my fingers, to take the carpeted stroll down salvation lane. I was already saved. She was not. Truth be told, I just wanted this madness to end. She rolled her big eyes again. Sometimes I felt I might could get lost in them.

Preacher called on my dad to lead the congregation in prayer. The deacons had anticipated fittingly. Dad savored this role and had a packaged prayer just for this occasion, not particularly dissimilar to his packaged prayer for grace, weddings, family gatherings, sick relatives, University of Georgia versus Auburn football games, and funerals ... for both saved and lost souls. It lasted a full five minutes with dramatic pauses and rejoining "amens" from the congregation. I thought this was worse than my Christmas Eve beating.

The song leader changed the invitation song to "Just As I Am. Page number 242 in your Baptist Hymnal." Blood washing had played itself out without the desired effect on the scoreboard. Time to send in the relief pitcher.

Thankfully Karen, a girl my age, thrice previously saved, walked the aisle confessing her three previous salvations did not take. I said a little too loud, "Thank God."

Several nearby godly parishioners, missing my sarcasm, shouted, "Amen," in response.

Georgia giggled. Mom, understanding, shot me a look. Jesus was not to be toyed with. I wondered how Preacher scored Karen's multiple salvations—long foul balls? I doubted it.

Finally, we were released and free to head for home.

Attached to the north side of our house was a covered carport where Dad stored his prized Ford Galaxy out of the weather. When we drove up from church that day, he uncharacteristically stopped short of the covering. Mom screamed. I looked out the front windshield.

There was blood everywhere. In the corner of the carport Jaws lay huddled, covered in blood and sand. Mom ran to him and scooped him up in her arms. Dislodging Sue from the back seat, she gently placed Jaws in my lap. The vet was closed today but he lived next door to his office. Mom grabbed Dad and flung him out of the car. We drove to the vet at breakneck speed. I rubbed Jaws' massive head, trying to reassure him everything would be okay, but I wasn't so sure. I did not know a dog had so much blood. It was pooling on the once blue, once brown, vinyl car seat.

Mom beat on the vet's door, rattling the adjacent window panes. He took one look at Mom's blood-covered Sunday dress, wiped his mouth with his dinner napkin and motioned for us to bring Jaws to his office. Mom carried him over. Jaws by now weighed close to 100 pounds. Mom weighed maybe 130. She carried him like he was a feather, gently placing him on the exam table. We expect our miracles to be grand, like Jesus raising Lazarus from the dead or Moses parting the Red Sea or the Braves winning the Series and, accordingly, I believe, just might overlook the everyday little ones. The vet's wife was also his nurse. She entered shortly and escorted us to the waiting room.

Mom was bawling and I felt I needed to stay strong. Mom put her head on my shoulder. After a while she stopped sobbing and straightened up. She wiped her face with a tissue and everything about her demeanor changed like flipping a switch. "Mom. You okay?" I asked.

She smiled. "Couldn't be better. Jaws is going to be just fine. I feel it." Maybe Jesus answered Mom's prayers.

The nurse walked through the door a couple of eternities later, covered in blood, but smiling. I took it to be a good sign. "Jaws lost a lot of blood but luckily no organs were hit. It looks like he was shot with birdshot," she added.

Mom nodded and smiled. I felt the rage building in my gut. For some reason, I had assumed Jaws had been hit by a car accidentally. It had not occurred to me someone did this to him on purpose. But I knew instinctively just who that evil someone was.

The nurse continued, "We need to keep Jaws overnight to give him fluids and keep an eye on him, but he is going to be all right. You can come back and say hi if you like."

We walked in. They had made an effort to clean Jaws up, but there was still blood on his fur, at least on the fur they had not shaved off. The shotgun pellet wounds were evident and plentiful. The vet had attached a cone about Jaws' neck to keep him from licking his wounds. He looked silly and, if not for the blood, I would have laughed. Jaws made an effort to lift his head and his tail wagged. Mom hugged and kissed him. I buried my face in his bloody fur and sobbed like I had not since the Christmas Eve Ham beating. I had been angry before but this was something entirely different ... I had hate in my young heart.

The vet looked at Mom and said one word, "Malvados." It was more a statement than a question.

Mom shrugged.

The vet said, "I can call the police."

Mom shrugged again and rubbed my head. "To what end?"

The vet nodded. Mom asked with a pained smile, "Can we put this on account?"

The vet smiled. "I consider this my duty. There is no charge."

Mom wasn't having this. She forced a smile. "Doctor, we ain't no charity case. We will pay you."

The vet nodded and rubbed his weekend stubble thoughtfully. He understood this was a pride thing. When you were poor, sometimes all you had was your name, your reputation. You guarded your reputation fiercely so as not to tarnish its luster. 'Cause once blemished it was very difficult to restore a reputation's shine. Being poor did not make your name more valuable—reputations are valuable to rich people as well. It was just that being poor meant it was likely your only valued possession and as such, guarded a bit more carefully.

"How about I get Doug to cut my grass in trade?" the vet asked.

Mom smiled a genuine smile. Bartering was acceptable. I think I may owe that vet a few yard mows to this very day.

On the drive home, Mom seemed oddly calm and began singing the invitation song, "Are you washed in the blood, in the soul-cleansing blood, are your garments spotless, are they white as snow, are you washed in the blood of the lamb." Her voice was not ethereal. It was an act. She knew not to fuel my dark heart and she had a plan to deal with this on her own. Mom dropped me off at the house and asked for my bat. I shrugged, but dutifully complied.

She tore out of the drive, spewing gravel, heading the few houses down to the Malvados' lair. I ran after her with Georgia shortly on my heels, barefoot but still in her Sunday best. Mom drove Dad's prized Galaxy in circles on the Malvados' front yard, artfully dodging the larger obstacles but with little regard to scratching the paint job. Old man Malvado came to the front door just as we made the edge of their "lawn." Mom got out of the car, bat in hand.

The man pointed a gnarled finger at Mom and asked, "What you gonna do with that little stick, old woman?" Mom was old to me but yet half his age.

Mom was silent as she fiercely swung only once at his knees, taking old man Malvado to the ground. I grimaced in sympathetic pain. He whimpered and spewed forth a series of words previously unknown to me. Mom could swing a bat. Maybe she could pinch-hit for Brian.

She whispered—no, more like seethed—wagging the business end of the bat in his whiskered face, "You and your kind stay away from my family."

Mom threw the bat to the ground and drove off not even seeing us. I ran up and retrieved the bat. It was a Hank Aaron Louisville Slugger, after all.

CHAPTER TWELVE

Mom was scaring me a little. Okay, more than a little. She had thrown caution to the winds, and that was unlike her. It was near four p.m., almost time to go back to church for Sunday evening service, before we walked back into the house. Mom and I were both covered in dirt, blood, mud and wrath.

Dad looked up from the dining room table. "Where is my dinner, woman?" To be clear, breakfast was called, well, breakfast. Lunch was usually lunch except on Sunday when we called it dinner. The evening meal was supper but on special occasions we called the evening meal dinner.

Mom smiled, washed her hands in the kitchen sink and opened a can of dog food in plain view. Typically, the dogs ate table scraps and leftovers, but we kept a few cans of dog food on hand for emergency. Dad watched her through a narrow slit in his good eye but wisely remained silent as she began again with the chorus of "Washed in the Blood." Mom placed the dog food on her good china and poured Dad a glass of iced sweet tea. She sat down beside him. "You gonna say the blessing, Dad?" she smiled.

I wasn't hungry, but I wasn't going anywhere. As a precaution, I slid the bat discreetly under the table. He was my dad after all and although he was firmly within the confines of my doghouse, I did not want to see his knees shattered like old man Malvado. Dad looked at me. "Go wash your hands, son."

I looked at Mom. I didn't know who to be scared for. "You hear me, son." It was not a question.

Mom smiled and I nodded. "You haven't touched your dinner," she said to Dad in a voice that sounded sweet but wasn't by any stretch of the imagination.

Slowly I pushed my chair back and made my way to the kitchen sink to wash up so I might keep an eye on any developments. "In the bathroom, son. What has gotten into you?" Dad roared. The kitchen sink was reserved solely for food preparation.

Dad was redirecting his anger on me, an easier target. Mom smiled and got up from the table clearing Dad's untouched dog food. She put on her "World's Best Mom" Mother's Day pink apron over her bloodied clothes, washed the dish, dried it and put it away in the cabinet. I left the bathroom door open to eavesdrop. I did not know what I would do should trouble break out, but I was clearly Team Mom.

Mom peeked around the corner. "Go ahead and take a bath, son, and put on your PJs. We will eat dinner in front of the TV watching the Magical World of Disney tonight while your dad is at church."

Walt Disney himself hosted the program on our only TV channel. The sixty-minute program started before we got home from church, so we always missed the beginning of the show. It was in color, but that really did not matter as our TV was a black-and-white. Brian boasted a color TV but it really wasn't. You could buy a multi-colored piece of translucent wrap to lay over the TV screen that added color to the picture, but the color made no sense. I gave Mom a forced smile. We never missed church. Dad started to say something but wisely thought better of it.

He stormed out of the house, slamming the screen door behind him. I expect he was heading to Granny's to get a sympathetic ear and a ham sandwich. On Sundays, he stayed dressed in his Sunday clothes. He would forgo the tie on Sunday night. Sunday evening service was a little more informal and even less attended. Mom often said Preacher could hold evening service in a broom closet. I think she secretly harbored a similar opinion of the windbag as I did.

I gathered my PJs and ran my bath. Dad had a hard-bristle brush on the ledge of the tub he used to scrub the oil paints from his dark skin, leathered by daily exposure to the south Georgia sun. I knew he worked hard to support us. I just didn't fully understand how much burden was on his shoulders. We did not have health care insurance. If anything were to happen to Dad and he couldn't work, we would be on the street in a couple of months' time. If we got sick, he could hold out a little longer by taking on some extra work. Dalton and most doctors were patient with us poor folks, knowing we would eventually pay them back. It was a disgrace to be seen as a deadbeat.

I used the brush to scrub Jaws' blood from underneath my nails and dried off with the cotton towel Grandma gave me for Christmas. It was my birthday present as well. There is a down side for having a birthday close to Christmas. After slipping on my PJs and tossing my dirty clothes in the hamper, the bed looked awful inviting. I thought I would lie down and take just a short nap before joining Mom in front of the TV.

In my sleep, Albert updated me with his remaining siblings. Jaws tossed his two cents in every now and then as well. Hope was always silent in my dreams. Jaws was exceptionally chatty tonight. I expected it was the pain drugs the vet had given him. I know the codeine medicine gave me some pretty crazy dreams. It's like your body is fast asleep but your mind is on fire.

Jaws showed me two of their brothers that lived with an old couple on the edge of town. The pups had been rescued not long after I found Albert and had been trained to be service dogs for the old couple. They lived a sweet life, were well fed, cared for and genuinely loved. They were not on my rescue radar. Tonight, though, Jaws showed me the old man. He was not well. It made me sad because I could feel the sadness of Jaws' brothers. They loved the old couple as much as the old couple loved them.

CHAPTER THIRTEEN

School was starting soon and I needed a haircut. Dad used to take me to the barber shop with him every other week. The barber shop in the South was a masculine sanctuary. Some of the old-timers sat in the shop all day discussing the news, as men spurned gossip, reading the papers and watching the grainy black-and-white TV sitting high on a shelf in the corner.

The shop, like most places, except the theater and the bank, had no air conditioner, and the entirety of the front of the shop was open to the street except on the coldest winter days. The floor was polished marble swept dangerously smooth a million times over with a straw push broom. A canvas belt powered a series of wooden ceiling paddles hanging overhead from brass fixtures that kept the air stirred and the temperature tolerable up until the dog days of summer, at least till noon or so. The barber shop smelled of talcum, disinfectant and Bazooka Bubble Gum. The barber chairs were chrome-and-leather mechanical contraptions that were reminiscent of the medieval torture chair I sat on during my sporadic forced visits to the dentist. I did not like the dentist. End tables sat between the wooden chairs and on these tables sat an assortment of magazines, men's magazines. Life, Time, Newsweek, Reader's Digest and the forbidden ones: National Geographic and Esquire.

Since the Christmas Eve Ham incident, I avoided Dad as much as I could. Hollis's barber shop was a good five-mile bike ride each way, uphill in its entirety in both directions. Science would suggest the last sentence to be untrue, but I challenge you to make the ride and come to a different conclusion. I woke early Saturday, skipped breakfast and completed my chores. Mom gave me a dollar for my haircut and a dime for the pay phone should an emergency arise. A pay phone booth stood watch on nearly every other corner at the ready for said crisis, or to call and check the time and temperature. I tucked the money deep into my front pocket beneath a tissue to make sure it did not fall out on my journey.

I fished a few brand-new Topps baseball cards from my collection—a couple of American League rookies I never heard of—and replaced the worn cards from my bike's fork. The cards did not get good mileage. Tens of thousands of dollars' worth of baseball cards were ruined in the spokes of my bike over my childhood days. Mom kissed my forehead, quizzed me on our address and phone number, admonished me to look both ways downtown and not take candy from strangers. Thankfully Hollis was no stranger. Steve was waiting at the ready at the end of the driveway. We mounted our metal steeds and headed up the hill to town.

Hollis did not take appointments; it was a first come, first served establishment. This was fine by most as it was an escape for the men from their wives nagging them to complete their "Honey-dos," or so I overheard. Most patrons would hang around for an hour or so before and then again after their haircuts. Saturday mornings were typically busy and today was no exception. Steve and I found a seat together at the back of the shop. Hollis winked at me as we walked by, acknowledging our place in the queue.

The shop was large with five chairs. Hollis had the chair closest to the door where he could feel the breeze, such as it was, and keep a watchful eye out on the street traffic. Hollis relayed the gossip, I mean news, of who was doing what with whom, amongst the shop patrons. Downtown Tifton on a Saturday was a bustling place. There was a lot of news.

The most junior barber had the last chair farthest from the street, and although the shop was packed, he sat idle in his chair. He stood and offered us a cut but I told him we were waiting for Hollis. Not everyone was skilled enough to give a boy a buzz cut. He mumbled something and flopped back down in his cracked leather chair expelling air making a fart sound. Steve and I laughed. He glared at us.

Hollis yelled out, "You boys okay back there?"

We nodded. Hollis yelled, "Catch," and tossed us both a piece of Bazooka Bubble Gum. "Watch your mouth, Smitty," he admonished the junior barber.

I bravely selected a National Geographic from the end table, anxious to explore the forbidden dark mysteries between its glossy covers. Hollis whizzed a piece of bubble gum at my head. I traded the National Geographic for a Time. The mysteries within must wait for another day to be discovered. I think Mom must have called ahead.

An hour passed and we traded seats a couple of times to get closer to the front door. The foot traffic was entertaining and the breeze comforting. Hollis alternated narrating the street scene with discussing crop prices and family health updates with the patrons. He called Mr. Adcock up to the chair and told me we were next. I smiled and nodded. Mr. Adcock was a town celebrity of sorts. He owned a series of flashy stores up and down the interstate that Mom called cheap tourist traps.

A lot has changed since Papi's youth. As a kid, it was darn near impossible for anyone with a physical handicap to navigate the sidewalk. There were no gentle ramps, reserved parking spots or cross signals. The handicapped were forced to traverse a difficult, if not impossible, obstacle course. So, it was a bit unusual when a wiry old woman showed up on Hollis's threshold pushing an even older man in a wheelchair. She banged hard up against the entry threshold but did not have the strength to get the chair up and over it. Steve and I got up and helped her over the obstacle. We were raised right. I pushed against the middle of the chair on the logo for Acme Medical Rental. Steve lifted up on the wheels. She gave us each a wheat penny from her change purse and a warm yellow smile. The old man grunted something unintelligible and smiled. I almost fell to the ground. I knew this couple. They were the old couple with Jaws' brothers.

The old couple were clearly known to Hollis, the barber. The old woman asked if Hollis could put him to the front of the line. No one objected, least of all us. This was great theater and if Hollis got distracted

I could yet take a peek inside the covers of the National Geographic.

She left the old man in the corner right by us and walked out. "I'll come collect him in a few."

I tried to talk to the old man but Hollis subtly nodded. I was in the chair when his wife gathered him and unable to interrogate her. "Who are those people?" I asked Hollis.

"Why you so interested in old man Gibbs?" Hollis answered.

"It's a complicated story," I answered. What was I supposed to say? *My dogs talked to me in my dreams.* Even I recognized that sounded crazy.

Hollis laughed. "I bet it is."

Other than their names, Hollis only knew the old man was really sick. "Probably would not last through Christmas." He said when I asked, "Dogs ... I don't know about any dogs."

Luckily for me Steve was an aspiring artist and had a photographic memory. Neither of those applied to me. I remembered the name Acme Medical Supply but not the corresponding phone number stenciled on the chair. When we got home, Steve tore a piece of paper from a notebook and started sketching. With a name, sketch and clue, maybe we could find this old man Gibbs and further reunite the pack. Steve hid his work in the crook of his arm as he furiously sketched, closing his eyes every now and then to picture the finer points of the old man.

Finally, after what seemed like endless revisions, Steve was ready for the big reveal. He flipped the paper to show me, exclaiming, "Voilà!"

I squinted my eyes and tilted the note paper one way and then the other. The sketch looked like the unlikely cross between a bespectacled Clark Kent and an aged Donald Duck. Frankly, not an altogether unlikeness, but I was pretty sure even the man's mother would not recognize him from the sketch. God rest her soul.

"That is helpful," I said to Steve—thinking, not at all.

I retrieved the phone book from the nook in the hallway and rifled through the yellow pages. The phone book contained two sections. The first section was the white pages, which included an alphabetic list of everyone in town who had a phone and their address. You had to pay an extra monthly fee *not* to have your number published in this book. To this day, that seems weird. The yellow pages were for business lines. Anyone that had a business line was published by type of business, then name, in this section. You could pay extra and make a bigger listing with pictures and an advertisement. This was a huge source of revenue for the monopolistic phone company AT&T. They owned the phone books, the lines and even the company that made the phones. It is no wonder Judge Green did his Solomon act and broke the phone company up a decade or so later. Acme Medical we found listed under the Medical section of the book.

"Look, there is Dr. Cohen's number." I pointed it out to Steve. Dr. Cohen had just a plain listing with no advertisement: Dr. H.J. Cohen, MD 382-5898. Steve shrugged. It was once considered bad taste for doctors and lawyers to advertise. For what it is worth, your Papi still considers it bad taste. My dad just had his number in the white pages as a residential line. Businesses paid more for a telephone line. Dad reasoned anyone looking for a sober painter would find him by word of mouth.

"Who is gonna call?" Steve asked.

"I'll do it." I dialed the number and the phone was answered on the third ring.

"Acme Medical. How may I assist you?" It was a woman's voice.

I panicked. I did not have a plan. "Is your refrigerator running?" I asked.

She giggled. "Well, yes."

"You better catch it then," I responded and hung up.

Steve looked at me perplexed. "What was that?"

I shrugged. "We need Georgia."

CHAPTER FOURTEEN

Steve entertained Georgia with my story. "Your refrigerator running? Are you ten?" She giggled at my expense.

It stung a little—okay, it stung a lot. Georgia's opinion of me seemed to matter and I was more than a little confused. Anyone else I would have just punched in the arm and said, "Shut up," unless Mom was around. I would have still punched them in the arm but I would have said, "Hush," instead. And Georgia, for goodness sake, could not field a ground ball for the love of all things holy. Why did I care?

Georgia looked at me funny. "You with us, Doug?"

"Yup. What's the plan?" I asked.

"I'll call Acme," she said confidently.

Steve gave her the number. I had already forgotten it. She dialed the rotary phone holding the receiver out so we could listen in. After three rings the same lady's voice answered, "Acme Medical. How may I help you?"

Georgia was flustered. "Do you have Prince Albert in the can?"

"What the h—" the detached voice replied.

"Prince Albert," Georgia replied, "Do you have him in the can?"

"No," she replied, clearly confused. Steve and I started laughing.

Georgia said, "Well, you better let him out." And hung up.

I started rolling on the floor in laughter. Georgia punched me on the shoulder. And told me to "shut up." It just made me laugh harder.

Grands, this likely makes no sense to you. As kids, we on occasion made random prank phone calls. This was a bad thing. There was no caller ID, so you could be anonymous. Prince Albert, along with being part of the British monarchy, was a popular product that came packaged in a can.

"That was your grand plan?" I asked. "And to be clear, you even messed up the prank. The lady said she did not have Prince Albert in the can. Epic fail, girl."

Georgia sighed. "I panicked."

"Maybe we need to work on a Plan B."

Jaws and Albert reported nightly. Old man Gibbs was not improving but we had some time. Both the pups were cherished and doing fine.

It was Thanksgiving break when Albert started panicking. We felt guilty we had put finding the pups on the back burner. Clearly, old lady Gibbs was looking for a home for the boys but could not find one. Old man Gibbs was about to pass and she planned on moving into an assisted living home that did not accept dogs.

Clearly, the phone thing was not a viable option for us. We felt a personal touch was in order. Problem was, Acme Medical was in Dog Island, not the best part of town, and a long bike ride. We decided we needed Mom's assistance.

Georgia started the conversation. "Do you trust me?"

Mom smiled. "Depends."

"Fair enough." Georgia continued, "You know I really like your son?"

"Wait—what?" I said out loud but it seemed no one heard me.

Mom said, "I do." As if Georgia had said the sky was blue, ice was cold, scrambled eggs need salt, or Jaws' farts were rank.

"And I would never do anything that hurt him."

"Okay, Georgia."

"And your son really likes me," Georgia continued.

"Wait—what?" I mumbled this time. Was this the whole "intentions" conversation?

Mom said, "Yes, I know he cares about you."

Wait—what? This time I don't think I said anything out loud. Did everyone think this? I liked the girl but "really liked" felt like a colossal leap. For sure I didn't feel the same way about her as I did Mom and the pack. And I loved them for certain.

"And we all love Albert, Hope and Jaws," Georgia continued.

Mom was growing frustrated. Clearly Georgia was stalling. "What is your point, Georgia?"

I was still stuck on she "really liked" me. But then again, Georgia loved the dogs and "really liked" me so I needed to put that in perspective.

"We need your help in rescuing two of the pack's brothers," Georgia blurted out and held her breath.

Expecting a strong argument or an objection, I grimaced. Mom replied, "I am in. So, what do you need?"

Georgia smiled. "For starters ... a ride."

We grabbed Steve. He had the sketch, such as it was. Mom gave us a ride to Dog Island and the modest offices of Acme Medical. The sign on the glass door said they were open. She parked by the door. "So now, what is the plan?" Mom asked.

"We go in there with the sketch and ask if they know this old man."

Mom looked at the sketch. "You want I ask if they know old man Donald Duck?" she deadpanned. I had never seen this side of her before. I kinda liked it.

Steve scoffed.

"You got a name?" Mom asked.

I said, "Gibbs."

Mom said, "Wait here." She snatched the sketch from Steve's hand, stifling a cackle.

She came back after what seemed to be an eternity.

"Well?" I asked.

"They don't have any clients with the last name of Duck." She could not hold back her giggle this time. "We need a plan B?"

"I think we are moving to plan C."

Steve took the sketch back from Mom and crumpled it. Georgia looked over. "It was a good drawing, Steve."

I chimed in, "Yeah ... of Donald Duck."

Georgia subdued a laugh. Steve's eyes narrowed. "Let's see you do better."

"Good point." I could not draw. My only really bad grade in school was penmanship. I could barely read my own writing after it got cold. Some things never change.

Steve opened the car door. "Where you going?" Mom asked.

"Let me try." He unrumpled his sketch and smoothed it out on the hood of the Ford. After a few minutes, he came back out.

"Well?" Georgia asked.

"They would not give me their number, but they took Doug's mom's number to give to the Gibbs."

"That is something," I said. "Did you show 'em Donald again?"

Steve crumpled the drawing and threw it at my head. I think the joke had overextended its welcome.

Mom sighed and tried to crank the Ford but the carburetor was flooded. This was not that uncommon. Grands, there were a lot of things in your Papi's youth that taught us patience. You just had to wait some things out a bit and try again, over and over, until you succeeded. Someone once said the formula for success is "Opportunity meets preparation." Papi's expanded formula for success is "Opportunity meets preparation, perseverance and hard work."

CHAPTER FIFTEEN

Albert kept us updated nightly on old man Gibbs's health. He was slipping fast. They were desperately looking for a home for the boys but had yet to find one. It was already Christmas break and the Gibbs lady had not called us. Mom called Acme. They had lost our number but agreed to call the Gibbs lady. It was New Year's Eve when we heard from her.

"Is this the boy with the Donald Duck sketch?" she asked Mom. It seems the Acme people had remembered our number but forgot our name. Thank goodness for Steve's art work. I giggled to myself.

"Yes, ma'am. Is this Mrs. Gibbs?" Mom asked.

"Yes, it is."

"How is your husband doing?" There was an awkward silence and Mom regretted asking the question.

"He passed," Mrs. Gibbs finally answered, her voice breaking. "He is in a better place."

Mom said, "I am sorry." She paused but pressed forward. "Did you find the dogs a home?"

Mrs. Gibbs explained she had "tried and tried to find a home for her boys," first with relatives and friends but they couldn't handle them. "They had grown quite large." Then she attempted several shelters, but they were all full. Ultimately, on Christmas Eve, she found a shelter in Putnam County that could take them both. She started crying. "But I am so worried."

"Don't be, Mrs. Gibbs," Mom said. "Give us the name of the shelter and we will go pick them up."

"I don't know if they are still there. It's a kill shelter," she whispered. Mom cupped the receiver trying to put the dark words back into the phone.

Mom got the name of the shelter and we looked up the phone number and called right away. It was long-distance so there would be a charge on the phone bill. Dad would be angry. We had to get long-distance calls preapproved through him. It was New Year's Eve. There was no answer.

I was worried of course but also relieved. We knew where the boys were and I was confident they were alive. Albert and Jaws would have "told" us otherwise. We just had to wait till January 2nd to go and pick them up. I looked forward to confirmation from Albert in my dreams. The confirmation did not come.

∞∞∞∞

We spent New Year's Day at Kenny's house—we being the extended family. In the winter, we traded in our baseball for a football and after lunch played a family touch football game in the side yard. The adults participated, which meant my dad would join. That kind of sucked the joy out of the game for me. I pictured Dad as Brian as a kid but without even a smidgen of joy. I was in no mood for Dad drama today. I got a glass of iced tea and pulled up a lawn chair in the shade to watch the game.

Dad would have none of this. "Get up and get in the game, son." Let mandatory fun time commence. I knew there was no arguing. I pushed a neighbor kid from the opposing team across the line to Dad's team. If I was going to play it would be on the opposing team.

For an old man of forty-something, Dad was a pretty good athlete. He played quarterback and actually diagrammed and ran plays in sandlot football. This was unheard of. I knew all his plays and his tendencies as to when he would call which play. The teams were evenly matched, and Dad's team was up a touchdown with the ball after a couple of hours of play. Unlike baseball, we did not have a definitive game completion time. We played till we didn't.

It was fourth down and based on the previous series of plays Dad called I knew he would call a crossing route and connect with Kenny when he crossed in to the right flank. I positioned myself correctly and intercepted his pass with no one but Dad between me and the goal line.

Dad was pretty fast but I had the momentum and easily was about to score when he yelled I had stepped out of bounds. Keep in mind the boundary was an invisible crooked line between a series of trees that bordered the lot. I knew there was no arguing his out-of-bounds call, but we had the ball with a first down and just a few yards from the goal. We would score easily and tie the game. But Dad immediately declared the game over, his team the victors, and led his team off the field of play.

I started to protest but remembered that would just cause trouble. My priority was recovering the dogs. Sometimes you have to take a loss to get a win. Remember that advice when you get married as it will serve you well. I congratulated Dad on his fair victory with all the sincerity I could muster ... which wasn't much. He missed the irony.

Steve asked, "What was that?"

"Gotta choose your battles, cousin."

CHAPTER SIXTEEN

Georgia met me at the screen door shortly after Dad left for work. "News?" she asked.

I shook my head no. "You?"

She bit her lip nervously and said, "No. Is no news, bad news?"

Georgia could read my mind. I was scared Albert was holding back and didn't want to share the news with us that his brothers had been put down. I could not bear the thought.

Mom called the shelter at nine a.m. sharp. She held the receiver tight to her ear so that we could not hear the other side of the conversation. She expected bad news as well. The shelter answered quickly. "Good morning."

Mom started to explain our story but was interrupted. "Yes, I am the Donald Duck lady," she said. She smiled and loosened her death grip on the receiver. Steve's wonky sketch had some powerful legs.

"We did have Mrs. Gibbs's boys, Pockets and Satchel, at the shelter. Mrs. Gibbs called and said you might be calling. Satchel was adopted by one of the workers here. She has a giant yard and big screened-in porch and three kids that adore Satchel."

"And the other one ... Pockets?" Mom asked.

"Well, unfortunately we could not find him a home and ..." Mom tightened the grip on the receiver again. Shortly she smiled, relieved at whatever the answer was.

"Can we get the phone number to that shelter?" Mom asked. Pockets had been transferred to a shelter in Sumter County. He had exceeded his stay in Putnam but the shelter workers said they just could not put him down. He was sweet, well trained and behaved. He was just so big they had trouble placing him, and the shelter was beyond capacity.

Mom turned her back to us and whispered, "Is that a no-kill shelter by chance?" She smiled. I assumed she got the answer we all wanted.

Mom relayed the good news. I was a little sad for Satchel getting split from his brother, but I was fine as long as he had a good home. It sounded like he did. Hopefully, Albert or Jaws would confirm it and put our minds to rest. I thought dogs were better off with humans but really, I was not sure. I mean, they were pack animals and we almost always split them up. I wasn't a big fan of my sister, but I know I would have been sad if someone split us up. And then there were cruel folks like the Malvados.

The only thing I was certain of was, us humans were a whole lot better off with dogs in our lives. They had a brand of love and loyalty that was different. There was no expectation or judgment. I could fart, not bathe, get a bad grade, strike out with ducks on the pond or wear mismatched socks, and the pack would still come lick my face and slobber on me. And they would be there to have my back even when I let them down.

No sooner had Mom explained the story to us than she was dialing another long-distance number to the shelter in Sumter County. Dad was going to be angry, very angry. I told Mom I would tell Dad I made the calls. I could take another beating. Mom teared a up bit and rubbed my head. "Don't be silly." Mom never got the switch after me again, although there was many a day I would have preferred it. Her disappointment was a thousand times more punishment than even one of Dad's beatings.

"Yes. We have Pockets. He is so adorable." She paused. "Let me see here … there's a note clipped to his file." Grands, there was time long ago when computers did not exist. People wrote stuff down on paper and placed those papers in files, which in turn were placed in filing cabinets. On occasion, someone would clip a note to that file with a metal clip known as a paper clip. Crazy stuff, right? Stay tuned. Next your Papi will tell you about playing something called board games and I Spy on long car trips.

"Oh, my. That Pockets is a popular fellow. Seems he has been scheduled for an overnight trial visit with a family in Tifton."

My sense of dread was alerted. "Really?" Mom asked. "Maybe we can visit him. We have three of his litter mates and had hoped to reunite them," she explained.

"Well, if the family doesn't take him, you are welcome to visit Pockets here at the shelter."

Mom could sense my concern. "Could you tell us anything about the family? Tifton is small town and I am sure we know them."

"I'm sorry. I don't believe it would be right to disclose that information."

I grabbed the phone from Mom. "Is it the cotton-picking Malvados? Can you at least disclose that?" I said angrily.

"Son!" Mom yelled at me and snatched the phone back from me. "I am disappointed in you."

I heard the lady on the other end. "Your boy seems quite disturbed. But I am afraid it is the Malvados."

Mom explained.

"Oh, my. Let me go and see if they have picked Pockets up yet. What is your number? I will call you right back."

I looked at Mom and shook my head, trembling in rage. "The Doug will not abide."

The shelter called back collect with our worst fears confirmed. The Malvados had just left with Pockets.

CHAPTER SEVENTEEN

Georgia and I flew out the door with the screen door slamming behind us. Mom was still in her housecoat and slippers. She ran down the hall to change.

I sprinted to the back corner of our lot and let out the emergency signal. *"Ca-caw. Ca-caw,"* I screamed through cupped hands. I crossed over to the opposing corner of our yard and repeated the call. Every able-bodied kid in the neighborhood knew to come running on the signal. It was our Bat signal.

Georgia was on her bike and holding mine at the ready. We stomped on the pedals standing the entire way to the Malvados. Mom yelled out the door to wait. We did not. Steve and Brian were coming up quickly from behind. Several of our other friends met us from the other direction. You could hear our Bat signal being relayed echoing through the tall pines in the distance.

Only Rusty was at home. He came to the door when he heard the commotion in his yard. "What y'all spole rich kids want now?" He stayed in the shadow of the door.

I started to go to the door and yank him out. Georgia stopped me. "Sometimes a woman's touch is what is needed."

I shrugged, annoyed. "Mom won't be here for another five or ten minutes."

Georgia punched me. "Me. Are you dense, boy?" She pointed both thumbs toward herself. She walked to the door, hips peculiarly swaying, with a faint smile on her face while flipping her hair. I thought she might be having a seizure. She was talking to Rusty in whispers and batting her big brown eyes like she was signaling him in Morse code. I couldn't make out what they were saying.

Steve and I kept a close eye on her in case Rusty tried anything, his elders made an appearance, or she fell to the ground shaking and drooling from whatever strange disorder she was experiencing. Brian held court in the rear. You never knew when that pride of marauding raccoons might attack our rear guard.

Finally, Georgia motioned me to the door. Rusty withdrew farther inside the shadows of the house. All the meanness and bluster seemed to have drained from him. He kept his eyes pinned to the dust-covered floor like he was reading from a script printed there. He sneaked a furtive glance at Georgia when he thought she wasn't looking. I wanted to punch him but saw that someone else had beat me to it. His left eye was swollen shut and he was missing about half his teeth. Rusty had taken a pretty good licking. Maybe that explained why he was helpful.

"They are meeting my uncle at Fulwood Park at high noon," Rusty explained.

"Why not here?"

"My uncle can't be seen with felons."

"What's a felon?" I asked.

Georgia punched me again. "Pretty much his whole family. Why you being so dense today?"

"Why you keep punching me?" I ain't never hit a girl. And Georgia was not going to be the first one. I ignored the pain in my arm. She had dug her knuckle into my muscle and it smarted more than a little. I turned back to Rusty. He was smiling at my discomfort but with the missing teeth he just looked creepy. "What they going to do with the dog?" I asked.

"They gonna sell the mutt to my uncle. He runs a weekly dog fight over in Adel. My uncle can't show his face at the shelters, so he pays us to pick up big dogs for him all over these parts." His voice held no remorse, no guilt, no shame. I stared at his face for a minute, wanting to finish smashing it. I wondered, are you born evil or do you learn it? Georgia grabbed my arm and pulled me away.

Our emergency alert system was primitive and flawed, yet effective in rallying the troops in a pinch. About half the kids brought assorted weapons. Water guns, bats and slingshots being the most common armament. One new kid, a Yankee, brought a long, curved stick I would later know was used to play a silly game on ice called hockey. Another kid brought a pack of straws and a notebook to make spitballs. An older kid who had a paper route brought a box of rubber bands and a homemade rubber band gun—a stick notched on one end and on the other a clothespin used as a triggering mechanism.

Kenny showed up in a Bulldog football helmet. He barked when I noticed him. Some kid I hardly knew was in full Atlanta Braves catcher gear and had a pocket full of firecrackers. Another had a bag of roofing nails. And yet another kid had two tin soup cans attached by a long twine cord. The other half of the kids brought snacks and boxes of imitation fruit juice. Altogether we had almost two dozen kids assembled in Rusty's litter-strewn yard with more en route.

Georgia lightly punched me on the shoulder and smiled. "You're on, kid."

It was my moment. I spent a few minutes explaining the situation. Our pack was beloved by the neighborhood kids—especially Jaws. He was a charming, handsome devil, the errant tooth and crooked smile complementing his eccentric character. And ain't none of us cottoned to dog-fighting. The kids were all in and ready to do battle.

I looked at Georgia, the only girl there. "You go stall Mom," I stuttered. "Divert her to Tyson Park." I knew Mom would wisely opt for a plan other than the irresponsible one I would conjure up. I am not sure if boys are taught to protect girls or it is innate, something hard-wired into our DNA. Either way, I don't think it's a bad thing. Women are thirty percent smaller than men and for a multitude of reasons deserve our respect and protection.

Georgia turned to Brian, prepared to delegate my "stall Mom" order, but before she could say anything he blurted out, "I got it. I'll go divert Doug's mom." I snagged Brian's slingshot and reached down and filled my pocket with some loose gravel from Rusty's yard.

I shook my head at Brian. Georgia shrugged. "It's his nature."

Rusty had explained to Georgia that the Malvados planned to meet the uncle in one of the lovers' lanes in the park. He wasn't sure which one. There were about half a dozen or so, depending on how you counted them.

We would have to send in a team to reconnoiter. Like I said, a few World War II movies had been watched. I picked out the six smallest and fastest of our platoon for this mission.

"You are not to engage the enemy," I explained. "Just locate and report back to the rally position at the Confederate monument." The marble statue could be seen from any point in the park except inside the shrubbery-walled lanes.

I pointed to PK and Zeke. "You two cover the points of egress. PK, take west, Zeke east." They stared at me, confused.

Georgia rolled her eyes and elaborated on my order. "PK, take the exit on Tift Avenue. Zeke, you take the one on Pence."

"Thanks, Sergeant."

Georgia corrected me. "Lieutenant." Without even knowing it Georgia was in the vanguard, the leading edge, of the women's movement in the late 1960s.

"Remember. No one engages the Malvados. Once you locate the enemy, report back to the rally point. I'll set off a firecracker." I looked at the firecracker kid in full catcher gear. "Hey, you, Joe Torre, brought matches, right?"

He adjusted his mask, patted himself down and pulled out a magnifying glass from behind his chest protector. "No, but I got this here."

"If you hear a firecracker, assuming Joe Torre can light one off, you will know we spotted the Malvados." I would have preferred he had matches but some kids were pretty skilled at starting fires by focusing the sun with a magnifying glass. Grands, don't try this at home.

"You scouts hightail it back to the rally point. PK and Zeke, you hold your positions and try and block their

escape, should they get through our lines with Pockets."
I gave them each half the roofing nails to spike the road.

"Questions?" I asked. There were none. "Let's ride."

My lieutenant informed me she needed to make a quick stop. I assumed it was to do whatever girls do in the bathroom that takes so long.

We made great time riding to the park on 12th Avenue in two long parallel lines. Mine was a motley army of the innocent, yet willing and brave. We knew every inch of the park—the lanes, the ditches and the playground. This was a more innocent time. The park was known for its azalea-lined lovers' lanes. Azalea bushes, left to their own devices, will grow to fifteen to eighteen feet. They were left alone. The lanes became these massive impenetrable tunnels that crisscrossed the park, blocking out much of the sun's light. There was typically only one entrance and one exit on each of the intersecting lanes … unless you really knew the park. We knew the park.

The park officially closed at dark and the police patrolled the road a few times each night to round up the errant high school teenager up to what Mom called "no good." Some of the older boys at church referred to parking at Fulwood after dusk as the "Submarine Races." Never could wrap my brain around that. The park did have a part-time resident. He set up camp in one of the rare oak trees that was located at a crossroads of the lanes. His tree-top camp was well hidden by the Spanish moss but we knew the park.

He was a wiry little red-haired fellow with a buzz cut and a full scraggly beard. One of those beards a bird could covertly nest within. His skin was deeply tanned and leathery. The most remarkable feature, though, was his eyes. They were a piercing crystal blue that seemed to penetrate inside your head. He appeared a little crazy but was harmless enough, at least to the innocents. Overall, he looked like a cross between a troll and a leprechaun. The pack had taken an immediate liking to him and they were good judges of character. We asked his name. He gave us a different one each time we saw him. We had taken to calling him Homeless Bob, or Hobo for short. He did not seem to mind.

Hobo's hidden treehouse camp overlooked a key intersection where I expected the Malvado meet to happen. The lane intersection gave multiple exit directions and was often frequented by other no-gooders doing business in the park. It was no small wonder that after this day the city cut the azaleas in the lanes down to about two feet high. It kind of ruined the park for us, but with time and perspective I understood why. It is almost always a handful of no-gooders that ruin things for everyone else.

I sent Steve to Hobo's camp with a couple of firecrackers, hoping to enlist Hobo into our quirky band of brothers. He wasn't much bigger than a kid, but he had a certain intimidating presence that made most people cross the street when they saw him coming. Steve would have to find a way to light the firecracker. Hobo frequently had a fire. If all else failed, Steve would give the emergency Bat signal: "*Ca-caw… Ca-caw.*" The rest of my motley platoon stood at the ready, nervously awaiting the battle to come. Suddenly I realized I missed Georgia at my side.

The Malvados drove an old dilapidated pickup truck of mysterious origins. They had welded several disparate body parts to a frame of unknown origin. The grill had a partial Ford logo devoid of vowels. One of the side panels had the remnants of a Cadillac emblem, the other a Chevy. The color was late-stage rust with faint patches of every hue in the rainbow. The windshield boasted a spidery crack to the point I was not sure how they could see to drive. One headlight and no taillights functioned. The cab of the jalopy was missing the seat, and in its place were three inverted five-gallon paint buckets. The truck would not be hard to miss. We had no idea what the uncle drove, but we expected it to be of similar ilk. We were wrong.

PK came screaming up on his bike, throwing gravel into us as he skidded to a stop.

"Why did you abandon your post?" I asked, learning this whole leadership thing on the job.

"News," he said breathlessly, "bad news."

"What?"

"The uncle..." —he gasped for air— "is a deputy sheriff."

"You are mistaken." It wasn't a question. My innocence had been rocked over the last year, but no way a police officer was involved in an illegal dog-fighting ring. There were a couple of officers who lived in our neighborhood and a couple more at church that I knew. Stand-up fellows all. I was not ready to accept that kind of evil from even a single person sworn to protect us.

"Naw." PK shook his head vigorously from side to side. "He saw me and yelled at me for being on the stone arch." There was a giant stone arch with a fierce winged gargoyle at its peak guarding the entrance to the park. "His name tag said Malvado. He is a deputy sheriff for Lowndes County. I don't think that is just a co ... co..." He could not come up with the word.

"Coincidence," I finished his sentence. Seemed doubtful for sure. "Good job, PK." I regretted distrusting him. I turned to the platoon. "Okay, you heard him. If you need to go home to mama, now's the time. The stakes just got bigger."

Joe Torre piped up, his fingers digging in his nose through the mask, "Ahh ... sir ... I don't like big steaks. Can I get a hamburger instead?"

PK laughed. I rolled my eyes. We had ample snacks. I sent a couple of the smaller boys to collect and organize the snacks for a picnic, in order to remove the kids from harm's way. The weight of leadership felt heavy on my shoulders.

"Sheriff Malvado, that dog-murdering no-good— he ain't going anywhere. I spiked his tires," PK said. I think PK might have just become a felon.

I grabbed the makeshift tin-can-and-string telephone from the kid who had brought it and gave it to PK. The homemade phone held no value as a communication device. "Fill these soup cans with sand and climb back to the top of the arch."

PK's face lit up with a mischievous smile. "I got it."

The other kid frowned. "Hey!" he protested.

I took one of the straws and a few sheets of paper and gave to him. "Your weapon, Private." Leadership is harder than it looked on TV.

Zeke came flying up on his bike. "Does anyone listen to my orders?" I mumbled. "I bet Patton didn't put up with this insubordination."

"The Malvados just drove in. Don't worry, I spiked the entrance but good."

I shrugged. Zeke's dad was also a housepainter and a deacon at our church. Yet still I did not know him well. He was always on the edge of our existence.

Zeke stammered nervously, "And now your mom's Galaxy is blocking the entrance with four flat tires." He held up four fingers as an unnecessary visual aid.

"Brian," I mumbled. A firecracker exploded.

"That's Steve," I said. The meet was at Hobo's camp where I expected. I dispatched four of my platoon south down the ditch to flank the meeting spot from the west.

"Pop out of the ditch once you go through the culvert. There is an entry to the lanes. Position yourself between the lane and the parking lot," I ordered. Two in the squad were armed with slingshots. One had a water pistol and the fourth would be shooting spitballs. "No one gets through with the dog."

"How do we stop a man with a gun?"

It was a good question. "Adapt, improvise, overcome," I advised.

The spitball kid stood at attention and saluted.

I returned his salute and added, "And don't get shot." I did not think a deputy sheriff, even a Malvado, would shoot a kid holding a plastic straw but the kid's enthusiasm was a bit frightening.

I sent half my platoon down Tift Avenue on bikes to get behind the enemy in the playground. There was no vehicle exit from this location. I planned to force the enemy into the playground, which had an open sight line to 8th Street traffic. Surely none of the Malvados would do anything crazy to us kids if exposed to the public. At least that was the plan.

I was fast running out of troops. To exercise the pincer movement, we would need to block all exits but the one I wanted them to take. I split the rest of the platoon into equal size groups, balancing the improvised weaponry among them. I was not sure I had enough troops to discourage the enemy from attempting to break through our advancing lines instead of retreating to the playground where the bulk of our forces lay in wait.

It was a cycling sea of pink ribbons, ponytails and frilly white blouses. There must have been twenty girls with Georgia at the front. The pack loped beside them slobbering, pink tongues dangling from the heat and effort. Reinforcements had arrived. In my excitement, I hugged Georgia. The girls giggled. I turned beet-red and could feel the heat rising up my neck.

Georgia pulled away and turned on a nearby faucet used for irrigation. The pack drank eagerly from the running water. "What is the plan, my captain?" Georgia asked.

"Major." I had given myself a battlefield promotion. She scoffed. I filled her in on the plan. She split the girls up evenly to go with my remaining troops.

"Weapons?" I asked.

Georgia smirked. "Our wits."

"That'll have to do," I said.

"Chaos is our friend." I gave last-minute instructions. "Create noise and havoc. The idea is to drive the enemy away from you, not to engage them." I stationed the boys with slingshots up front just in case any of the Malvados needed a more tangible barrier.

Georgia and I headed off, taking a shortcut to Hobo's camp, the expected location of the Malvados. We were going to try and sneak up to Steve and survey the battlefield from an elevated position.

CHAPTER EIGHTEEN

A battle plan typically falls apart once the conflict starts. Ours, even before that. Steve had been discovered and was hog-tied to the same tree as Pockets. Pockets was bravely positioned in front of Steve, alternately licking his face and growling and snarling at the Malvados. His growl was impressive.

Old man Malvado said, "See, I told you he would make a good fighter for you." The old man spat on Pockets. He was in negotiation for more money with the deputy sheriff. They were passing a bottle of whiskey between them. It served as an analog for a microphone of sorts. The man with the bottle had the podium and spoke, took a swig, and handed the bottle to the other. It was a strange but effective ritual. Then again, strange is subject to perspective. I don't think they were eating human flesh or washing in blood.

I heard the troops advancing noisily down the lane. The Malvados did as well. "What the Sam Hill is that?" the sheriff asked but with words a bit more colorful. He fished out a crisp twenty-dollar bill from his tethered billfold. "As agreed upon." He handed old man Malvado the whiskey bottle and went to grab Pockets.

Pockets bared his teeth and snarled. The sheriff reached for his nightstick and was greeted by a barrage of flying pebbles. He swiveled on his heels to face the airborne gravel onslaught. The sheriff was wearing dark aviator sunglasses. They were immediately covered in a wall of slimy spitballs. Fountains of water joined the barrage of pebbles, firecrackers, spitballs and the high-pitched squeals of young girls and prepubescent boys. The younger Malvados fled in the direction of the playground. I smiled. I loved it when a plan came together.

The fog of war creates confusion. That was our plan, chaos and confusion. Georgia sneaked around and untied Pockets. I got to Steve, but before we could make our escape, the sheriff grabbed both me and Georgia roughly by the ear. Pockets growled and bit into the sheriff's ankle.

Steve fled as Kenny charged into the sheriff, helmeted head down, driving hard into his no-nos. He gasped and fell to his knees, releasing Georgia from his sweaty grasp. Georgia ran pulling Pockets with her, but Pockets escaped her hold and ran back into the fray. The sheriff still had a firm grasp on me. I looked up to see my army turning the corners and advancing from all three directions. A motley army of defiant brave kids here to save a dog.

Mom and Hobo were surprisingly at the vanguard of the troops coming from the south—she, armed with my Hank Aaron autographed Louisville Slugger, Hobo with a smile. His smile exponentially more terrifying than Mom's bat. I did not see Brian. I rightfully assumed he stayed with the car to protect it from an improbable pride of marauding raccoons. Joe Torre was bent over a stump trying to light a long string of firecrackers with his magnifying glass, made more difficult by the shade in the lane.

Old man Malvado saw Mom with the bat. The sheriff saw Hobo's freakish smile. The sheriff said, "It's time to make like a tree and leave."

He released me, secured Pockets by the collar and hightailed it toward the playground. Joe Torre set off the string of firecrackers right beside me, temporarily deafening me.

Mom mumbled something, shaking me by my shoulders. I looked at her dumbfounded. She seemed concerned.

"We are a bunch of peculiar chickens?" I asked. It is what I heard her say. It did not make sense.

Everyone laughed. She smiled. "No, son. I said you are bunch of peculiar children."

I nodded. That we were, there is no doubt, but we had work left to do. We ran into the breach, screaming, the furry pack in the lead followed by Mom, Hobo and the remainder of the Peculiar Chickens.

Once we hit the lane's opening into the playground, we noticed traffic on 8th Street was at a standstill. People were exiting their cars and lining the park, observing the bedlam within. Four girls swung from the maypole, bright pink flashes lashing out at any Malvado that dared come within range. Two of the bigger boys from our platoon were on the seesaw bouncing off a subdued Malvado on either side. The monkey bars had been turned into a makeshift prison holding several of the Malvados, their hands lashed with pink ribbons and guarded by slingshots, adolescent insults and the rubber band gun.

Pebbles and spitballs sailed in all directions from the spinning merry-go-round indiscriminately striking both friend and foe, encouraging everyone to stay low. The Yankee stood on top of the slide launching pine cones with his curved stick at anyone that moved, with remarkable accuracy. Joe Torre had mercifully exhausted his supply of firecrackers deafening me in the lane. He ran around in ever-narrowing concentric circles, his eyes skyward, looking for an imaginary foul ball to catch. Even I recognized that boy needed help.

All of the Malvados were subdued except the sheriff and the old man. The pack encircled the two, low-growling and snarling, their backs arched with the fur along their spine spiked high. The sheriff, holding fast to Pockets by his collar, started to reach for his service revolver with his free hand.

Hobo screamed with barely a whisper, "Look around, Sheriff." There were at least a hundred people lining the playground watching the drama play out. "You gonna shoot a bunch of kids in front of an audience?" You had to strain to hear Hobo's words but at the same time you needed to cover your ears from their intensity.

"No, but it is within my rights as a sworn police officer of the great State of Georgia," he raised his free hand in the air like Preacher, "to shoot a pack of rabid dogs." His mouth smiled but his eyes did not.

Georgia walked up, pulling Hope, Jaws and Albert away. "Your move, Sheriff."

Old man Malvado broke and ran, waving for his family to join him. Hobo held up a single finger. No one moved another step.

Hobo was an unusual sight. A small man who spoke softly but carried himself with freakish confidence bordering on terrifying. The sheriff started moving again in the direction of his parked police cruiser. "You will get the dog when I get safely to my car."

Hobo wagged his bony finger. "Not going to work that way, Sheriff. Might want to listen to little man here." The sheriff froze. Hobo waved me forward.

"I got men—" I started to say.

"Soldiers," Georgia interrupted. "Boys and girls."

I gave Georgia my best scowl and continued loudly. I was still half deaf from the firecrackers. "I have men … soldiers, boys and girls,"—Georgia was in my head and I was getting a bit redundant—"stationed between you and the car. Let Pockets go and we will give you safe passage back to your cruiser." That was a fib. I had no way of calling off the squad in the ditch or PK on the stone archway. He would just have to suffer a few more injuries to his ego on his retreat.

The sheriff released Pockets, turned and scampered away, attempting to appear casual in his retreat but missing the mark. He looked like an Olympic speed-walker with a full load in his britches. Old man Malvado broke and ran, showing remarkable agility. Albert stood on his hind legs with his giant front paws on the old man's shoulders and wrestled him to the ground.

The Peculiar Chickens laughed and yelled, "The Grizzly!" recognizing Albert's signature move. The old man's pants turned dark as he peed in fear. Albert released him without any real harm, but I unleashed a round from my slingshot catching him square in his nonexistent behind as he further attempted his damp escape. He jumped, turned and scowled but kept running, his kin on his heels. I had not promised the old man safe passage.

The ditch squad saw the sheriff was without Pockets and gave him free passage. PK had waited over an hour in the hot sun at the top of the arch with two cans of sand and a long string attached to the gargoyle. There would be no safe passage from PK. We ran back to observe. Dozens of spectators abandoned their cars and scampered to follow. This was great theater. The sheriff slammed his cruiser into reverse, immediately flattening three of his whitewall tires on the scattered roofing nails that salted the parking lot. He ignored the flats and peeled out, skidding toward the stone entrance. PK timed it perfectly, unleashing both soup cans heavy with dirt. They arched into the windshield shattering the glass.

The cruiser veered off and hit the arch, knocking PK and the stone gargoyle twenty feet to the ground, breaking PK's right arm. The gargoyle smashed through the windshield and landed in the sheriff's lap, pinning him between the seat and the steering wheel. Two stone-cold monsters sat face to face.

The old man had parked his dilapidated truck nearby. About two dozen Malvados piled in the cab and the bed of the truck like drunken circus clowns. He avoided the roofing nails but plowed into the back of the cruiser, spilling out Malvados left and right. I heard sirens in the distance. Someone had found a pay phone and called the police.

Ultimately, PK and the gargoyle were our only casualties of the Battle of Fulwood Park. The Malvados were much less fortunate.

CHAPTER NINETEEN

The next day we rode to the hospital to visit PK. We signed his plaster cast. PK went to the window and waved at our newly enlarged pack: Jaws, Albert, Hope and Jelli. They howled in delight as PK enthusiastically waved with his good hand.

PK asked, "Jelli? I thought the new pup's name was Pockets."

I explained the night before. "He earned his new name." The new boy was super-jealous of any attention not directed toward him. He had slept on top of me to ensure he was closer to me than Jaws.

"What I miss?" PK asked.

Brian filled PK in on all the details of the battle of Fulwood Park, none of which Brian witnessed from inside the safety of Dad's Galaxy. We had found him in the back-seat floorboard with the doors locked, cowering beneath a blanket, wearing his new baseball cleats and batting glove.

I started to protest. Georgia pulled me back. "Let him have this. He needs his participation trophy," she whispered.

"A celebration of mediocrity?" I shrugged. I thought "mediocrity" kind. One day, I hoped, someone would recognize that even second place is first loser, much less awarding trophies to the clover harvesters in right field on the worst team in the league.

Georgia placed one hand on her hip and shook her head slowly from side to side. I deserved her look of disapproval. Brian and even Rusty had been dealt a bad hand. Whatever I might have endured as a kid was nothing compared to what they suffered. That whole perspective thing again. I might not have shoes but I had feet and all my teeth ... well, except one. Maybe I wouldn't have played their lousy hand any better had it been dealt to me. Having a tough childhood is no excuse for being an insufferable jerk as an adult, but it should at least earn a kid a little empathy.

Brian rambled on to PK detailing his nonexistent role in the Battle of Fulwood Park. I smiled. Georgia squeezed my hand and smiled back.

"So, what became of the Malvados?" PK asked.

"The police arrested the sheriff for drunk driving and the old man for drunk driving, child endangerment, driving an unlicensed vehicle and public urination." Brian was if anything a fountain of knowledge.

"Well, at least there is that. But how about the dog-fighting ring?" PK asked.

Steve was waiting for this moment. He flipped open a satchel filled with hand-printed flyers. He must have stayed up all night. "We mail these to all the dog shelters and police in the area. At least we can cut off the Malvados' supply of dogs and alert the authorities."

We each took a flyer from his hand. They were in the style of an old Western movie wanted poster. Across the top in bold letters was "WANTED." The next line read, "Old Man and Sheriff Malvado for ILLEGAL, IMMORAL and IRRESPONSIBILE Dog Fighting." Steve was a big fan of alliteration. Beneath the lettering were two almost identical drawings of Donald Duck. We burst out laughing, Kenny literally rolled on the hospital floor.

The floor nurse came and told us we were "not supposed to be back here." She smiled and winked but shooed us out anyway.

PK looked down at his newly adorned cast as we left. At the top, just above where we signed it, Georgia had drawn a heart and written "Georgia" and "Doug" within its boundaries. Beneath the heart she wrote, "Long Live the Peculiar Chickens."

The End

Je Suis

Acknowledgements

Peculiar Chickens is a work of fiction. That said many of the stories within the book were taken from my life growing up in South Georgia in the Sixties. Steve and Kenny are my very real cousins, and in my youth, were my, mentors, best friends and constant companions. The real Brian, Malvados and Preacher (not their actual names) added color and drama to my early years and without those experiences I would have a lovely but dull story. My Mom, who is no doubt an angel, was my rock. I miss you Mom. My dogs Albert, long since passed, and my current serial farting companions, Jaws and Jelli. My beautiful wife Jenn who encouraged and supported me and played a key role as a sounding board and final editor in writing this book and getting it published. Thank you all.

Author website: dmalonemcmillan.com
Twitter handle: @EzekielANovel

CPSIA information can be obtained
at www.ICGtesting.com
Printed in the USA
FFHW020710091218
49810268-54325FF